Death in the Dark

FELINES OF FAIRYTALE FOREST
BOOK TWO

K.L. MONTGOMERY

Cover design by the author, made with images licensed through DepositPhotos.
Paperback ISBN: 978-1-949394-80-1

Published by Mountains Wanted Publishing
P.O. Box 50
Harbeson, DE 19951
mountainswanted.com

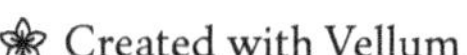 Created with Vellum

A double life, a dark secret and a disappearance create another wild ride for Cat and the Felines of Fairytale Forest!

At the Fairytale Forest amusement park, there's been a shakeup in the management. Cat and Gloria are getting used to their new manager, who tasks them with training a new custodian. Meanwhile, the park's feline exterminators continue to wage war over disputed territories.

When a park employee goes missing, of course Cat and Gloria were the last ones to see him. Cat is once again thrust into the role of amateur sleuth. At least this time she knows Zoe and her clowder have her back.

Missing Security Guard Kevin Morris appears to be leading somewhat of a double life. Can Cat, Gloria, Zoe and the gang follow the clues to solve the case of his mysterious disappearance? Or did Kevin's secrets lead to his untimely demise?

Murder by Moonlight is the first book in the Felines of Fairytale Forest cozy mystery series. Visit a southern amusement park full of fantasy creatures and feline exterminators and meet Cat, a tenacious fifty-something custodian, and her spirited coworker Gloria. These ladies just can't resist a good mystery. Follow the clues and solve the case alongside Cat, Gloria and the whole furry gang!

Map of Fairytale Forest

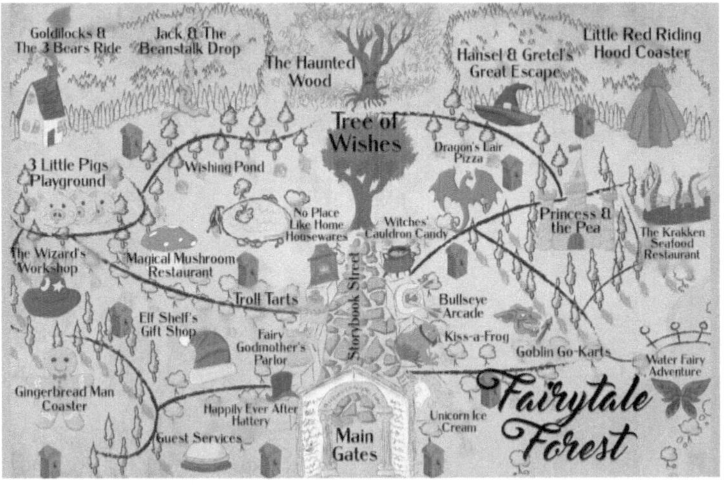

Designed by Kadan Knapp

To my sons, who taught me everything I know about Dungeons & Dragons, which is admittedly not that much, but enough to give me the idea for this book. So there's that.

Prologue

Hooded eyes gazed out across the Ashley River, narrowing into thin slits as the news anchor droned on and on about how Fairytale Forest was reopening now that the person responsible for the murder of one of their employees was safely behind bars.

"Hopefully, it will be smooth sailing from here on out for the Lowcountry's favorite amusement park," the co-anchor quipped with a plastic grin.

"Not if I have anything to say about it!" the mastermind growled, cracking their knuckles loudly before they turned off the television set.

"One victim wasn't enough to get the park shut down, but never fear. There are plenty more people I can have murdered. And the perfect victim is next on my list…"

One

ZOE

"The Water Cats are in danger," I announced to my clowder as we gathered for our nightly meeting. The park was emptying out, and it was time for us to begin our hunt. First, we went over old business. Then new business.

Then we would move on to our own business—catching tasty rodents. *Mmmmm.*

"Water Cats?" Mr. Cool Cat's head jerked up from where he had been licking his hindquarters.

"Yeah, the ones that live over by the river," I specified, though it was perfectly obvious which cats I was referring to.

"River Cats," Cool corrected me.

"River Cats, Water Cats—whatever!" I tried not to get exasperated with Mr. Cool Cat. He was the senior member of our clowder, and he deserved respect. But he had been a little off lately, and I was getting worried about him.

But I was even more worried about this clowder that lived on the banks of the river that flowed through Fairytale Forest. They nestled in the marshy reeds and seemed to enjoy chasing frogs and eating fish right out of the river.

"What's up with them?" Ice wanted to know.

"What do you think is up with them?" I tapped my paw on the ground impatiently. "What is the number one problem in this park?"

"Um, not enough mice to go around?" Ziti ventured.

"No." I tapped my paw in double-time. Why were they playing stupid with me tonight? I didn't have time for stupid—not now, not ever.

"The bipeds are always sending us new mouths to feed?" Amber was still missing the point, leading to triple-time paw tapping on my part.

"Scar!" I bellowed so loud, the ears of every single feline in the vicinity immediately flattened. "Scar thinks he runs this joint, and he's making life miserable for the Water Cats or River Cats, or whoever they are this week. They are a skittish bunch as it is, and he's taking advantage of them."

"What do you propose we do about it?" my brother, Moony, asked. As he spoke, Ziti padded up to his left side, while Priss, otherwise known as Princess, flanked his right side. These two were making me itch like a bad case of the fleas.

And my brother seemed to be eating all their attention up.

"I don't want him taking control over there," I explained. "It's too close to our boundary. And I don't want him taking advantage of cats who haven't done anything wrong and mainly keep to themselves. They deserve life, liberty and the pursuit of happiness, the same as we all do."

Ice cocked his head. "The pursuit of what now?"

"A very famous biped said that," I explained. "I saw it on the History Channel." I looked over my crew.

Hank was probably not going too far tonight. But Ziti, Amber and Ice looked like they were champing at the bit to get out of here. Sass and Daisy were tormenting a cricket. And Cool was looking for another way to argue with me. That left my brother and his little harem.

Sheesh. It's going to be a long night.

"Be thinking of a solution to the Scar problem," I concluded our meeting. "Okay, you're on your own tonight. Happy hunting!"

I had my own agenda to pursue.

CATHERINE

"Well, what do you think of the new boss so far?" I asked my coworker and bestie, Gloria, as we headed for our carts.

She didn't get one word out of her mouth before the new boss, Sheri, marched up to us, a petite figure with dark hair pulled back in a long ponytail on her heels. "Ladies, this is Nora. She is just starting tonight. I want her to shadow the two of you for the rest of the week. Make sure you explain what you're doing and answer any questions she has."

"Sure thing." I dipped my chin in acknowledgment of my boss's order. Actually, Sheri was my boss's boss. Karen, our immediate supervisor, took a leave of absence once Sheri was hired. Sheri was replacing the former director of facility services, Walter, whose wife had gotten them into a wee bit of legal trouble a few weeks ago, which led to his resignation.

That sucked for us because Walter was a great boss, and change was never fun. Especially when you're a "seasoned" worker like myself and Gloria.

We were finishing up the busy summer season, and Sheri was super gung-ho like a lot of new managers are. I didn't *dislike* her exactly, but I wasn't a fan of being micromanaged. Especially not when I'd had this job for approximately a million years. At least that was how long it felt sometimes.

After Sheri turned down the hall, I opened the back door of the facility services building and ushered Gloria and Nora out into the thick, humid August air. It was so thick, in fact, it almost hurt to breathe.

"I'm already soaked in sweat, and we just got started." Gloria pulled at her vibrant floral tunic. "This is stickin' to me worse than a frog on fresh asphalt!"

"It's not the heat." I nodded in solidarity. "It's the humidity."

Nora just stood there watching us, her pale blue eyes flicking back and forth between us like she was watching a tennis match. Maybe she wasn't from the South.

"Nora, did you hear me ask Gloria what she thought of the new boss?" I tried to force her to talk.

She shook her head instead of giving me a verbal answer.

Oy. This is gonna be a long night.

"Well, come on, Nora, we're gonna start with the courtyard bathrooms. That's always the first job of the night. Then we move on to the tree."

She nodded this time, showcasing her full repertoire of communication skills.

If I hadn't just touched a trash can, I would be facepalming myself right now.

Some chatter carried on the humid night breeze around the building. I flashed Gloria a look, and she nodded. It was nice that we had worked together so long, we usually didn't need to use words. Unlike Nora, though, we'd spent a full decade learning about each other before we moved to the look and gesture stage of communication.

"Jayden!" I shouted toward the group responsible for the chatter. Riotous laughter erupted—like someone had just told a very funny joke. I called Jayden's name again as soon as the sound died down.

Three heads swiveled toward me, one of which belonged to Jayden, youngest son of the park owners, the Forests. "Hey, Cat, Gloria!" He grinned as he said goodbye to his friends and made his way toward us. "How goes it?"

I watched Nora carefully to see if she would react to Jayden, who was a very handsome young man. The eighteen-year-old would be a freshman at the College of Charleston, leaving us at the end of the month when fall classes kicked off. His gaze drifted over to her, but she refused to make eye contact with him.

Oh, dear. Well, maybe she's not into men?

Jayden's gaze bounced back to me, and he almost imperceptibly tilted his head toward Nora as if to request an introduction. I didn't want to put her on the spot, but I couldn't very well stand here and not introduce them either.

"Jayden, this is Nora, one of our new custodian employees. Nora, this is Jayden Forest." I didn't add the part about him being the owners' son. He would be finishing his seasonal employment stint soon, and Nora was likely one of the new hires brought on to take the place of summer temps leaving at the end of the month. She'd probably only be working with Jayden for a week or two.

Her pale blue eyes flashed over at him, and the tiniest smile appeared on her face and then vanished again like a frightened ghost.

"Nice to meet you, Nora." He reached out his hand to shake hers, and I held my breath, wondering if she would be brave enough to perform the social nicety. I felt bad for putting her in an uncomfortable position, but even working night-shift custodial, we had to be social once in a while.

Whew. Her hand darted out to limply shake his and then went right back to the pockets of her denim cut-off overalls. She was such a cute girl—long, toned legs. Glossy dark hair. Pale skin and those wide blue eyes.

"What's on the agenda tonight?" Jayden rubbed his hands together in anticipation.

"Showing Nora the ropes as we do our regular routine." With that, Gloria nudged Nora toward the cart, and they headed to the women's restroom to start the cleaning process.

Jayden waited until they were out of earshot. "She seems very shy."

I sighed as I watched them disappear inside the building. "Yeah, I kind of wonder how she got through her interview."

"Dad said, after the murder, applications are down. He might have been scraping the bottom of the barrel." He pulled a face and shuddered. "I'm outta here in a couple weeks, but this has been a fun summer. This is a great place to work, and I think I can say that pretty fairly. I didn't get any special treatment as the bosses' son."

I patted him on the back. "No, of course not. Your parents are very fair." I wondered briefly about Sheri being hired to replace Walter after Jayden's scraping-the-bottom-of-the-barrel comment.

"Hopefully no more murders while I coast through these last couple weeks!" Jayden grinned.

"Fingers crossed," I said, equally flippant. It took a special kind of person to joke about coworkers being murdered, like the kind of person who makes a career out of cleaning up bodily fluids.

"WELL, WE DID THE BEST WE COULD," GLORIA COMMENTED AS we headed toward the employee exit at the end of our shift. Dawn was breaking, and a red glow was rising up between the trees in the distance.

"I'm sure Nora will loosen up as the week progresses. It was her first shift, after all. I caught her laughing at my jokes a couple of times." I hit the button for the gate and waved to the security guard on duty.

"Yes, I'm sure your stellar sense of humor will be what coaxes her out of her shell," Gloria mused, patting me on the back.

"Well, I tried to entice her with Jayden, but that seemed to be a non-starter." I sighed.

"Good evening, ladies." The security guard tipped his hat at us as we made our way through the gate.

"Who they got working security tonight?" Gloria squinted as she peered into the booth.

"Hi, Ms. Bress. It's me, Kevin Morris." The guard was a young man, likely in his early twenties, with sandy-brown hair and a thick mustache. I wasn't sure what made this younger generation think mustaches were cool. *I guess they weren't around for the 70s...*

"Well, have yourself a blessed day, Kevin." Gloria grinned and waved as we passed through the gate and headed out to our cars.

One thing I loved about working at Fairytale Forest: it was more of a family than a workplace. Just like a family, it didn't mean you would necessarily like everyone, but most folks were down-to-earth, honest, and would do their best to make your shift go by as fast and pleasantly as possible.

Two

"**M**oony, are you listening to me at all?" I hissed at my brother.

His back arched, then his ears flattened as he turned his head to look at me. "Scar…Water Cats… yada yada…"

I stomped my paw on the ground. "Exactly! You're not listening to me at all, ya meat ax!"

"Meat ax?" He shook his head at me, then his eyes wandered off toward the clearing where two cats were prancing around, their tails waving proudly in the air.

Of course. It was Ziti and Priss. It was like they were having a flirt-off to see who could capture my brother's attention. If cats rolled their eyes, I'd have a headache from doing it so many times.

He was forcing me to stop playing nice. "Quit staring at those idiot mollies and pay attention to me, or I'm going to put you on Mr. Cool Cat duty for a week, you hear me?"

That did it. His whole body whipped around to face me now. "Don't threaten me with hanging out with that old geezer. I swear, if I hear one more story starting off with, 'When I was a kitten...we had to chase mice uphill both ways!'" He changed his voice to imitate Cool's raspy meow.

"Look, he's not going to be around forever, and he's the closest thing our clowder has to a parent," I reminded him. We all had a soft spot for Cool, but he could be quite cantankerous in his old age.

Moony crossed his paws and gave me a look that said, *you can't be serious right now.*

"What? It's true."

"You're the only parental figure we need, Zoe. Putting up with your constant nagging is hard enough without having someone else boss us around. At least Cool doesn't try to do that, though he does always think he's right. And the way they did things back in the olden days was the best, you know."

I sat up on my haunches, my tail beginning to twitch with annoyance. "Who makes sure this clowder stays fed? And on the Wrangler's good side? And who defeated Scar and Vinny just a few weeks ago in the epic battle over Priss?"

Moony's whiskers twitched. "Epic battle? Sis, you have delusions of grandeur."

"Delusions of grandeur?" I spat. "Who taught you *that* phrase?"

"You're not the only one who has access to information," he sneered. "You may have been educated by the television, but I have a more powerful teacher."

"Oh yeah?"

"Yeah, it's called the internet." He turned his back to me

and took a few steps away, his tail waving as if he was proud to get the last words.

"Internet!" I scoffed, or the closest thing a cat can do to a scoff. "You can't read!"

He threw his head back over his shoulder. "Turns out, you don't have to!"

About that time, Priss and Ziti got tired of him ignoring their little show. They came sashaying our way, swinging their hips, their eyes glowing in the dark. Night had finally settled over the park now that the crowds had cleared out. The only bipeds around at this hour were the security crew and cleaning crews.

Which reminded me—I hadn't seen my acquaintance Cat in a while. She was one of the cleaning bipeds and helped me win that forementioned epic battle.

"I just wanted you to know that I'm planning to rendezvous with the Water Cats at some point in the near future. Vinny has been over there talking to them about some sort of alliance, and it smells fishy to me."

"Mmmm…" Priss purred, "fish!"

"Not the good kind of fish, though they are apparently quite talented at catching them from the river," I explained.

"I'm in," Moony stated.

"Me too." Ziti head-butted him and then rubbed up against him. To his credit, he did not encourage her.

But he was enjoying this attention too much, and I was afraid the constant distraction of Ziti and Priss competing for his favor was going to get him in trouble. It wasn't like he didn't already get captured thanks to Scar, Vinny and their goons.

"I'm going hunting." I pointed my paw at the massive tree in the middle of the park. It wasn't a real tree—it was one of the park's attractions. "Meet me back here when the moon is over the tree."

CATHERINE

I finished showing Nora how to restock her cart from the supply room, and we made our way out of the facility services building toward the courtyard, where Gloria was pushing her cart toward us. As we grew closer, I could tell she was nearly bursting with energy. Her sixty-something-year-old legs were practically jogging.

My work bestie wore a Kelly-green tunic and leggings with a palm frond print, and her hair was wrapped in a matching scarf. She always looked so cute at work, and I looked like someone auditioning for *Sweatin' to the Oldies* with Richard Simmons.

"What's up? You look like you have tea to spill," I joked, using a phrase Jayden taught me.

"Tea? Why, I'd never spill tea on purpose!" She gasped at the audacity. "But I do have gossip."

"Well, don't hold us in suspense, right, Nora?" I was making an effort to include our trainee, but she was so quiet, I sometimes forgot she was with us. I needed to pay more attention too, lest I say something I didn't want her impressionable young ears to hear.

The young woman just smiled and nodded.

Well, I was trying, anyway.

Gloria didn't waste another second. "I just came from

cleaning in the security office, and I overheard them talking about Kevin Morris not showing up for work tonight."

I shrugged. "So?" That didn't seem like as big of a deal as she was making it out to be.

"Well, apparently someone saw him earlier today at Wal-Mart, and he wasn't sick or anything. And he didn't call in. That's apparently very unusual for him," she explained.

"Maybe he caught a fast-acting bug at Wal-Mart. I mean…" I didn't need to state the obvious, right?

Nora let out the very tiniest giggle.

"This is Kevin, who we saw last night when we left the park, right?" I clarified. "The security guard?"

"The same," she confirmed. "He's worked here for four years and apparently has never missed a day."

"Ever?"

She shook her head. "They said never ever. And there was no answer when Derek tried to call him."

"Huh, well, I hope he's okay. He seemed like a nice guy." I remembered our previous night's conversation. It wasn't extensive or anything, but he seemed friendly and smiled at us. He always seemed to be chipper when we saw him.

"Yeah, they said he is super quiet and shy but very reliable," Gloria continued. "I wonder where he could be. Never missing a day of work in four years is pretty impressive."

Before I could add my two cents, the strangest high-pitched squeal came out of Nora's mouth. We both whipped our heads toward her. She was staring at something in the bushes, completely mesmerized.

She pointed, her mouth agape, the high-pitched sound still coming out.

The bushes rustled, and a furry creature sauntered out, shaking her tail like she'd just woken up from a nap. She strutted toward us, her long fur waving in the tiny bit of breeze that was making it almost tolerable to be outdoors this evening.

"Oh, that's Daisy," I explained. "She's a pretty girl, huh? A long-haired calico." I almost added that Zoe claimed Daisy was dumber than a box of rocks—good thing I stopped myself just in time.

"Kitties?" Nora squeaked, her entire face lit up with joy.

"Yes, the park has cats. They didn't tell you that at orientation?" Gloria asked. "They're feral cats, used to control the pests in the park. We aren't supposed to interact with them." She flashed me a look that said, *Except for you, who can communicate with one of them.* But, of course, we couldn't tell the new employee that.

"Kitties," Nora sang, a dreamy quality to her voice. "I want them all." Without a doubt, it was the most words we'd ever heard her utter consecutively.

She started to walk toward them with slow, almost zombie-like steps. Like she was in a trance.

I went to pull her back toward us when another voice shattered the peaceful evening we were enjoying. "Catherine and Gloria?"

Fortunately, though her name was not called, Nora was as startled by the voice as I was. She took her place next to me, and I didn't even have to jerk her away from the fluffy calico who had taken one look at the newcomer and marched right back into the bushes. *Can't say I blame her.*

Our new boss was approaching, hands on her hips like she was about to scold us. "Hey, Sheri, what's up?" I spoke on behalf of all three of us.

"Catherine and Gloria, I need to see you right away in the Security Office." She had a stern look in her eyes, like we might disobey her. What were we, naughty children? "Meet me there in five minutes."

"Okay." I nodded, and so did Gloria.

"What should I do?" Nora asked meekly as Sheri made a beeline for the Tree of Wishes in the center of the park. The massive structure held several levels and was used as the main station for the park's sky tram system, while the security office was underground where the "roots" of the tree would be. There was also another security office and a secondary office for the park owners at the very top of the tree. Both offered breathtaking views of the park.

"Well, first of all, don't interact with the cats, okay? Go empty those bins in the alley between the restrooms and No Place Like Home Housewares, and we'll radio you when we're done. It shouldn't take long," I instructed.

"Are you guys in trouble?" she squeaked out, her voice as soft as a mouse's. Well, if a mouse could talk. And maybe they could—I could apparently communicate with animals now?

"Who, us?" I elbowed Gloria, and we both broke into uproarious laughter.

Whatever we'd done, we'd weasel our way out of it. I had no doubt.

DEREK SWIFT WAS WAITING FOR US IN THE SECURITY department's conference room, which was high-tech and sleek-looking, like maybe it was inspired by one of those Star Wars or Star Trek shows. I wasn't a fan of either franchise, but it had that sci-fi vibe to it.

I'd already had a run-in with Derek, suspecting him in the murder that happened in the park a few weeks ago. He was a chronic mansplainer and apparently had a violent streak, so I wasn't a big fan of his, and I was pretty sure the feeling was mutual. He sat next to his departmental secretary, and, of course, Sheri was there too. They were all scowling.

Couldn't wait to find out what this was about.

"You were the last two people to see Kevin Morris," Derek stated. It sounded an awful lot like an accusation. Was this his idea of retribution?

I looked at Gloria, who shrugged, and then we both looked back at Derek. "Um, okay?"

"We have you guys on camera leaving the park at the end of your shift last night. You spoke to Kevin. We don't have audio, just the video. He clocked out and went home right after that."

"I'm sorry," I said in my nicest, most congenial tone, "but so what?"

"He's missing," Derek continued in his patronizing tone.

I noticed Sheri didn't have our backs here. She didn't ask Derek to tone it down. She just sat staring at us with her short, spiky dark hair, which looked blue on the ends from the cool LED lights above us.

"We didn't have anything to do with him going missing," I stated firmly. "Why on earth would you think we're involved?"

"I didn't say you were involved," Derek seethed, "but now that you jumped to that conclusion, I have to say, my suspicions are aroused."

The way he said "aroused" made my skin crawl. *Ew.*

"You were the last ones to talk to him on property," Sheri

finally jumped in, and I could only hope she was going to get to the point so we could get on with our work. We didn't exactly have The Spanish Inquisition on our to-do list for tonight, you know?

"What did he say to you?" Derek demanded. His hand resting on top of the table clenched into a formidable fist.

"Um, pretty sure it was something earth-shattering like 'have a good day.'" I rolled my eyes. "Trust me, it was just small talk. He didn't give any indication that he was planning to disappear off the face of the earth." If they wanted to play nasty, I could certainly play along.

Keeping his steely gaze trained on me, Derek lifted a remote into the air and pressed a button. A screen dropped down out of the ceiling with a whirring sound, and then a video began to play—no audio.

It was Gloria and I approaching the security booth. Ugh, I remembered my earlier thought that I looked like part of the *Sweatin' to the Oldies* cast. I was smacked in the face with the realization I looked even worse than I thought.

Getting in and out of the park with ID cards was a relatively new development, as the Forests were just entering the twenty-first century when it came to such measures. I swiped my card, and Kevin tipped his hat and spoke to us. Then Gloria spoke, and then Kevin spoke. Finally, Gloria told him to have a "blessed day." I remembered that part, and told our interrogators as much.

"We're all smiling and clearly having a normal conversation," I insisted. "I don't know how anyone could think otherwise after looking at that footage."

Derek harrumphed. "Well, it still doesn't clear up what happened to Kevin."

"Well, no," I agreed, "but we can certainly keep our eyes

and ears open. The custodians are all over the park. We see and hear a lot of things."

"Thank you, Cat and Gloria." Sheri stood up. "That's all for now. Don't forget to go through the checklist for Nora's training. Back to work!" She clapped her hands for emphasis.

If I was mildly ambivalent about our new boss before this experience, the pendulum was now swinging toward outright disliking her. From the way Gloria murmured a Gullah proverb under her breath, I had a feeling we were on the same page as usual.

"What did you do to Derek, anyway? He really doesn't seem to like you." Gloria pointed out as we stepped out of the tree and headed for our carts. I would radio Nora when we got there.

"A big fat nothin'!" I sighed. "He should know better than to make enemies of the custodial staff. There are all sorts of ways we can make his life miserable."

"Yeah, like not emptying his trash," Gloria retorted.

"I can think of worse stuff than that." My mind rumbled with all the evil possibilities. "I think we should go ask the cats if they know anything."

"The cats, huh?" Gloria's eyes sparkled. "Think you can still communicate with them?"

"Well, I definitely intend to find out…"

It had been a huge shock the night we discovered the dead body on the main street of the park. But we didn't just stumble upon it. The colony of cats that helped keep the park clean—I liked to think of them as our department's feline partners—ushered us straight to the body. And I found that I could hear the lead cat, Zoe, speaking to us.

I thought I was going crazy at first. Then I realized she could understand me too.

I would say it was the start of a beautiful friendship, but with cats being aloof and self-centered, I'd say we had developed more of a business relationship. I was eager to find out if we were still in business, so to speak.

Three

CATHERINE

Before Gloria and I could wheel our carts to our next assigned duty area, the detective we'd worked with on the previous case emerged from the tree. I couldn't remember her last name at the moment thanks to middle-aged memory deficit, but I did remember her first name was Shelly, and I was proud I'd managed to stash that nugget in my overstuffed memory container.

"Hey, Detective." I left my cart and ambled over to her. Gloria followed. *Is she here about Kevin? Already?*

She looked up from the small yellow legal pad she always carried and met my gaze. "How may I help you, Ms. Lyons?" She hadn't forgotten *my* name. But she probably had it written down somewhere, which was an unfair advantage. She was also probably five to ten years younger than me.

I decided to cut to the chase. "I was just wondering what

kind of leads you had on Kevin's disappearance. Does anyone in the park have any ideas?"

She frowned as she looked down at her notes and then back at me. "Unfortunately, no. Everyone in Security said he was very quiet, punctual, and reliable. They said he didn't seem to have much of a personality and never talked about his family or his interests outside of work. They just kept repeating how shocking it was that he didn't show up. Evidently, he had a long streak of perfect attendance."

"He's always been friendly to us," Gloria contributed. "But we never said anything more than hello and goodbye in passing."

"I'm getting the impression no one here knew him well," the detective said. "I came here first because this was the last place he was seen. He lives alone, so no significant other or roommate to question. I guess my next stop will be his parents' house. They live out on Johns Island. And then I'll talk to his neighbors and landlord."

"Sorry no one here had any info for you." I watched her scribble a few things on the legal pad. "I heard someone saw him at Wal-Mart after his shift."

She scribbled that down. "Do you know who?"

I shook my head. "Sorry, that was just a rumor—not even sure it's true, to be honest. I was hoping not to see you again. No offense."

She smirked. "None taken. I know the police prowling around one's workplace has to be pretty nerve-racking. I don't blame you for not wanting to repeat the events of a few weeks ago. Hopefully Mr. Morris will turn up soon." She handed both of us a business card. "Please reach out if you find anything that might be useful to our investigation."

I stuffed the card in my front pocket. Oops—forgot to

look at her last name. But at least I could see it later and give myself another opportunity to forget it. "Oh, I do have a question."

"What's that?" Her eyebrow quirked as her eyes drilled into mine.

"Don't they usually wait forty-eight hours before beginning a Missing Persons investigation?"

She shifted her weight from one foot to the other. "Yes, but Derek thought it was fishy that Kevin didn't show up tonight and didn't answer any messages. Derek used to be on the force—we went to the academy together. I owed him a favor, so I'm looking into it now."

"Oh, okay. Is Derek the one who called it in, then?" I didn't know why I was asking, but curiosity had gotten the better of me.

"Yes. He also said another park employee brought it to his attention that Kevin hadn't responded to texts or phone calls. So…he gave me a call."

"I understand. Well, thanks for coming out here to the park again." I gave her a smile, and she dipped her chin at us both before heading down the path toward Storybrook Street.

I waited until she disappeared from view before walking back over to where Gloria and I had abandoned our carts. "Well, what did you make of that?" I asked my comrade.

"I wonder what employee mentioned it to Derek. Seems like she ought to have been speaking with that person, right?"

"I was thinking the same thing. Now that's fishy to me. And Derek used to be a cop—but that doesn't surprise me."

"A lot of security folks are former police or wannabes," Gloria pointed out.

"Let's go talk to Zoe," I suggested, "if we can find her. I'd like to know if she and her cats know anything about Kevin."

ZOE

I didn't have a biped wandering around calling out my name on tonight's bingo card, but that was what I heard just as I was getting ready to head over to check on the Water Cats, or River Cats, or whatever the fluff we were calling them these days. I had already been interrupted about fifteen times, so it didn't surprise me that my biped associate, Cat, had now earned a spot on my Hiss List.

I stepped out of the bushes and gave her my best scowl. Which likely looked like a normal feline expression to the bipeds, but at least I was giving some sort of warning that I was in a foul mood.

"There you are!" came her excited shout.

"Shhhh! Do not attract attention to us," I reminded her as I backed into the bushes. Anyone stumbling upon this scene would probably think Cat was talking to a bush. I was fine with that illusion.

"Hey, I need to talk to you." She crouched down, using her cart and her biped colleague to shield her. "Where's a good meeting spot?"

"The castle?" That was our previous meeting spot, or did she forget? Plus, it was on the banks of the river, near the aquatic felines' encampment. I needed to ask them their preferred name when I finally got to meet with them.

"Right. Heading that way." She nodded, giving her colleague a dopey smile. Bipeds were so easily amused and entertained.

She and Gloria weren't exactly known for their speed, so I knew I would beat them. Did I have time to talk to the Water Cats first; that was the question?

I gave her a curt nod, and, with a flick of my tail, I was off, scampering along the perimeter of the cobblestone courtyard to make my way over to the castle. As soon as I arrived in the vicinity of the river, I detected a foul stench that could only come from one of Scar's henchmen. Likely Vinny—my nose rarely failed me.

I didn't want to get into it with that mousebrain before talking to Cat—he would only make my mood fouler—so I raced into the castle, hoping none of the thugs saw me. Perhaps I could ambush them after this meeting was concluded, scare them away from the Water Cats for good.

I heard the bipeds' custodial carts rolling on the sidewalk and knew their arrival was imminent. Amusingly, they thought they were being stealth, but I heard every single one of their steps.

"Zoe?" Cat's voice echoed off the ceiling and bounced around the cavernous space inside the castle.

I sauntered out, my tail waving like a plume. "Hello, Cat."

"Long time, no see," she greeted me. Her colleague gave me a little wave and an obnoxiously toothy grin.

"What can I do for you?" I sashayed over to a tapestry depicting the story the castle was based on—something about a princess and a small green legume. *Bipeds are so weird!* I sharpened my claws while I waited for Cat to get down to brass claws.

"We have an employee missing," she stated.

"Okay?" I stared at her, blinking slowly.

She took a seat on an ornate wooden bench, and her colleague sat next to her. "Do you know anything about the security guard named Kevin Morris?"

"Is he related to Morris, the famous feline from the Nine Lives commercials?" I was in a mood tonight, wasn't I?

"How do you know about him?" Cat asked, her curiosity apparently piqued. Gloria elbowed her and asked her what I said. Then Cat translated for her.

This conversation was going to take all night if it was going down like this.

"Never mind." I waved a paw at them. We felines passed down our history from generation to generation, but I didn't expect the bipeds to understand our culture. "To answer your question, yes, I know him."

She glanced at Gloria, nodding, and then back at me. "What's he like?"

"He's quiet to the other bipeds, but he's a giant turdcicle to my kind." An image of Kevin flashed in my mind, his towering height and cheesy mustache, as Cat relayed my response to her colleague.

Gloria's hands flew to her face to cover her mouth as laughter spilled out. Cat snickered and then followed up with, "Turdcicle, eh? That is quite original. What did he do that gave you that impression?"

"He likes to harass us with his flashlight," I explained. "I don't fall for it anymore, but many a feline has just about gone mad trying to chase the light."

She relayed this to Gloria, and they both chuckled. "Anything else you know about him?"

"Yeah," I answered, relishing the opportunity to vent about one of my least favorite security bipeds, "his girlfriend broke up with him, and he's been particularly cruel since then."

"Girlfriend?" Cat seemed surprised. She told Gloria, "He seemed like such a loner, I'm surprised he had a girlfriend."

"She works here too," I continued, trying to get this conversation wrapped up so I could get on with my own agenda. "At Dragon's Lair."

"Dragon's Lair? Here in the park?" Cat confirmed.

"The pizza joint." I licked my lips. "Sometimes they leave whole pizzas in their dumpster out back. Attracts the mice, which are easy pickins', and then there's cheese and pepperoni for dessert." Just thinking about it was making my stomach growl.

"Yum!" Cat laughed. "Do you happen to know her name?"

"Bree," I answered without any hesitation. "She likes us. She leaves treats for us sometimes, even though that's strictly forbidden."

She seemed satisfied with my answer. "Ah, okay. Well, that's more info than we had before. Anything else you can share?"

Gloria was tapping her foot because Cat had stopped translating for her. Good. Maybe I'd get out of here sometime this moon cycle.

"That's all I can think of right now."

My ears perked when I heard a shrill cat-fight sound that made my fur stand on end. "I gotta scram."

"No problem. See ya around, Zoe!" Cat waved as I leaped

into action, bounding out of the castle and back onto the pathway in the direction the sound had come from.

I PRIED MOONY AWAY FROM HIS TWO ADMIRERS TO CHECK ON the Water Cats. I wanted to find out what they preferred to be called after Cool told me they identify as River Cats. Everyone's identity was important, and I didn't want to mis-clowder anyone.

We stealthily waited in the reeds, surveilling the cats who lived in the marshy banks of the branch of the Ashley River that flowed through the park. My brother and I were not fans of water, so it was hard to understand how they could be happy living right next to it, but, hey, we weren't here to judge. They were a quiet, peaceful group, unlike Scar and his Mafia Cats.

Speak of the Devil...

None other than Vinny and his associate Alfie were prowling around the area.

"We're not gonna let them take advantage of these inno-cent felines," I said to Moony.

My brother puffed out his chest and gave a solemn nod. "What do you want to do?"

"Let's run them off. We'll just run straight at them, full-speed. Maybe we'll get lucky, and they'll fall into the water. There's nothing more humiliating to a cat than getting all wet!"

"Sounds like a plan, Sis. Give me a signal."

I tapped my paw once, twice and then hissed, "Go!"

We sprang out of the reeds and bounded like we were

chasing prey, ambushing Vinny and Alfie and sending them hurtling through the air in shock. It was easily the funniest sight I've ever seen, these two scaredy-cats, one tuxedo and one fat gray short-hair, sailing into the night sky. One of the bipeds in Security showed me the "cats and cucumber" viral video that went around the internet a few years back, and it was just like that.

Freaking priceless!

"Go on, scram!" I yelled once they landed on their feet, shaking it off like it never happened.

They scampered away, hackles raised and eyes wide. Moony and I shot each other a victorious look, then we noticed a half dozen pairs of glowing green eyes staring at us.

"Oh, hi! I'm Zoe, and this is my brother, Moony. We're part of the Courtyard Clowder. We came over to pay a goodwill visit and noticed you had some likely uninvited guests."

The cats just stared at us like they didn't know how to communicate.

"Uh…do you know the southern feline dialect?" I asked.

One cat stepped forward. "I'm Delta, the leader." She was a gorgeous tortie with dark brown and orange patches and wide hazel eyes. "Beck and Brooke are my seconds." They were both small, wiry pale-gray tabbies, almost silver under the moonlight.

I stood my ground and spoke in my leader voice: "Pardon me for being ignorant on such matters, but we have a difference in opinion on whether you are the Water Cats or River Cats."

There was silence as the cats who greeted us were joined by a half dozen or so more cats, and they all sort of started moving with their paws and tails and whiskers and mouths. They weren't speaking... It almost looked like they were dancing and doing a lip sync routine—I knew what that was from watching TV with the security guys.

Moony brushed up against me. "What in the world are they doing?" he whispered under his breath.

"No clue. Be polite," I warned him.

Finally, Delta broke away from the group and turned to face us again. "We are the River Cats," she announced like they just had a meeting to choose an official name.

"Oh, okay," I answered. Moony nodded. "Good to know. Well, it's nice to meet you."

"The pleasure is all ours," she returned.

Now that we had that out of the way—Cool was right, I suppose—I'd get down to business. "The two cats who were just here—Vinny and Alfie—have they been giving you trouble?"

She conferred with the other cats in their strange almost ritualistic dance and then returned her attention to us again. "Those cats you mention...they are villains, no?"

"Um, yeah, you could say that." Moony's chin moved up and down in the affirmative. "They're bad news for sure."

"We got that impression. They threatened us." She sat up tall with Brooke and Beck flanking her.

My eyes widened. "They did? How?"

"They said if we don't pay them a weekly tax of fresh fish from the river, then they won't protect us from the rogue felines who are attacking various clowders in the park," she explained.

Moony erupted in laughter. "Yeah, the rogue felines are him and the rest of Scar's thugs."

"We wondered if that is the case." She sank to her belly and crossed one paw over the other.

"Don't worry. We're not going to let them bully you," I assured her. "We are just over in the courtyard if you need anything. In the bushes near the big tree."

"Okay," Delta said. "As a thank you and show of good faith, allow me to give you a parting gift."

She stepped over to the rushing water, jumped out onto a rock and then waited, her paw poised over the stream. The current was strong thanks to recent rains. She studied the water and then, fast as lightning, her paw darted into the current, and when she pulled it out of the water, a fish was speared on her claws.

My brother and I both had to pick our jaws up off the ground. "That's an amazing trick!"

"One for you," she said, tossing the fish toward me, and, within another minute, "and one for you," she said to Moony.

"Well, thank you!" We both licked our lips. As much as we liked mice and other rodentia, fresh fish was a real treat!

Four

"Are you sure Sheri isn't going to have an issue with you using the computer in the supply room?" Gloria's eyes darted nervously around the room, which was filled floor-to-ceiling with metal racks holding cleaning products, toilet paper, paper towels, and other supplies. The pungent odor of industrial-strength chemicals permeated the air.

"You act like we're committing corporate espionage or something," I teased her. "Since when are you Miss Goody-Two Shoes?"

"You know what my *binyah* would say, right?" Gloria gave me a sharp look with one eyebrow arched. I loved hearing her Gullah expressions, but I needed to get this done stat.

"I'm not sure, but this old white girl just wants to figure out what happened to Kevin." I shrugged and went back to hacking into the computer.

"Hacking" was definitely an exaggeration. I wasn't too keen on technology—or, I should say, technology didn't seem too keen on me. But I had produced two sons who worked in techy fields, so there had to be some know-how in there. I just needed to search the employee database to find out who worked at Dragon's Lair Pizza and on what shifts. I had never heard of anyone named Bree, but there had been a lot of new-hires for the summer.

"Ah, here we go!" I clapped a little too loudly, and Gloria looked like she was going to have a conniption fit. "Relax, Gloria, I'm in." My fingers flew over the keys—I learned to type on an actual typewriter, a mid-80s IBM model, to be precise.

"Hurry up!" Gloria screeched. "I hear someone coming!"

"Eureka! Breeanne Townsend—she works the early shift. YES! She'll be coming in right as we're leaving."

Gloria made some weird noise like a bird—a shrill "cuckoo, cuckoo!" and I immediately stepped back from the computer, my heart pounding in my chest even though I knew I wasn't really doing anything wrong. We used that computer to notate when more supplies needed to be ordered.

"Everything okay in here?" Jayden poked his head in. "I heard a weird noise."

Right behind him peeked a small, meek face. *Nora. Hmmm...*I wondered what happened to her after she studied under our tutelage. We'd encouraged her to spread her wings and fly from the nest, and apparently she flew right into Jayden's arms.

Well, maybe not his arms, but she appeared to be following him like a shadow. They made an adorable couple, and it wouldn't be a bad idea to hitch your horse to the Forests' cart. That was one heck of a swanky cart!

"Hey, Jay! Hey, Nora!" I grabbed a bottle of bleach off one of the shelves behind me. "How's your shift going?"

"Oh, you know, same old. Have you guys heard anything about Kevin Morris?" Jayden asked. "My parents are afraid the park is going to come under public scrutiny again if this guy isn't found soon."

"We're working on it." I tilted my head toward Gloria so it was apparent what I meant by "we're."

"Oh, good! He'll be glad to hear that. I know how much you guys helped out with the...thing before." He winked.

Oh, good. He didn't say the word "murder" in front of Nora. Smart boy.

"Well, we've gotta get a few things done before we clock out. We just needed some more bleach." I flashed a beaming smile.

"Yeah, we've gotta restock too, right, Nora?" He turned toward her, and she gave a small smile.

Why did I have a feeling they were not in there to restock in the...ahem...traditional sense?

Gloria insisted on dragging our carts over to Dragon's Lair Pizza because she wanted us to look like we were still working. I rolled my eyes, but I knew there was no arguing with her. When that woman's mind was made up about something, it was impossible to make her change it. She probably had a Gullah saying about that too.

I knocked on the back door where supplies were

unloaded and trash was taken out. It didn't smell too appetizing back here, and the kitchens weren't in use yet, so no delectable pizza aroma was available to counteract the yuck. I spotted Carlos, the manager, right away.

"Hey, Carlos, good morning. How's it going?" I dipped my chin at him as I stepped into the kitchen with Gloria on my heels.

"Do y'all need something?" He stood with his fists on his hips like he was already exasperated, even though his workday was just beginning.

"I wondered if Bree Townsend has clocked in yet? I need to talk to her a sec." I smiled pleasantly and hoped my confident tone would yield positive results.

"Yeah, I think she just got here. She should be in the prep area." He pointed to a long, gleaming stainless-steel counter on the other side of the kitchen where two workers stood decked out in black-and-red striped aprons.

We headed over to where a tall, gangly teenage boy with patchy facial hair and pimples stood slicing tomatoes and a short, curvy young woman with purple, teal and royal blue hair that ran down her back in two braids chopped onions. When she turned to look at us, she wiped her forearm against her eyes, which looked teary and red-rimmed.

Oh—was she sad about Kevin?

"Hi, Bree?" I got her attention before she went back to chopping onions.

She laid down her knife and spun to face us. "Um, yeah?"

I ran my fingers through my thick gray waves and gave her a non-threatening smile. "Hi, I'm Cat, and this is Gloria. Do you mind if we ask you a few questions?"

She wiped her hands down the front of her apron, then pulled a tissue out of her pocket and blew her nose. *Ugh. I'll remind her to wash her hands before she starts chopping onions again.* "Um, I guess so."

"Do you know Kevin Morris?" I began, noticing her light blue eyes filling with tears again.

She sighed. "Yeah, why?"

"I'm sorry if I'm upsetting you," I apologized, noticing she was going for the tissue again.

"I'm not upset. I'm chopping onions," she stated matter-of-factly.

Oh, right.

"Okay, well, anyway, not sure if you've heard, but he's missing, and the police are looking for him. I heard you used to date him."

She rolled her eyes. "Yeah. Whatever."

"Do you have any idea where he might be?" Gloria joined the chat.

Bree scoffed and rolled her eyes again. Then Tomato Guy turned around. "She doesn't want to talk about Kevin," he informed us.

"Oh." I bit my lip, trying to figure out the best way to gather some more intel. So far this interview was a bust. "Sorry, I don't know you. I'm Cat, and this is Gloria."

"Yeah, I heard you before," he replied rudely.

"Did you know Kevin?" I pressed. We were past time to clock out at this point, and the Forests hated overtime. We were going to get in trouble if we didn't get this wrapped up soon. Bree had already gone back to her onions, and I didn't get a chance to remind her to wash her hands. *Double ugh!*

"Not very well. I know he's off on Thursday nights because he's an SC, and that's when they play," Tomato Guy said.

"SC?" My eyebrows arched as I studied his pimply face. I

wasn't sure how old Kevin was, but this kid couldn't have been older than seventeen.

"Ship captain," Bree supplied, still not turning around.

"Ship captain? Like on a boat?" I questioned.

They both laughed. Gloria and I stared at each other. Kids today sure were weird.

"No, it's a game," Tomato Guy said, still chuckling. "They play on Thursday nights at the game shop in Charleston. It's called Prisons & Pirates."

"I see. But you don't have any idea why he's gone missing?" I tried to circle back to the reason we were here.

They both shrugged.

"You haven't spoken with him, Bree?" I probed a little deeper.

"Look, he dumped Bree for some girl in his P 'n P game," Tomato Guy said. "So maybe leave her out of this?"

Bree threw down her knife, and it clattered against the stainless-steel counter. Then she ran off down the narrow aisle between the sinks and ovens, disappearing down a hallway.

Tomato Guy sneered, "Great, see what you did? You upset her!"

I sighed and shook my head. Well, we had gained a little info. Gloria laid a hand on my shoulder, and when I met her gaze, she tilted her head toward the clock. It was 6:15. We needed to skedaddle.

I scooped up the onion and tossed it into a nearby trashcan, and then we hightailed it out of there.

"Hey!" Tomato Guy called after me. "Why'd you do that?! You owe us an onion!"

ZOE

I'd about had it. After I heard what Scar and his thugs were trying to do to the River Cats, I decided to take matters into my own paws. I knew I shouldn't confront him on my own, but Moony was busy chasing mice with Ziti, Hank was passed out under the bush, Ice and Cool were doing who-knows-what, and I hadn't seen the rest of my clowder all night.

I made my way over to Scar's territory, my fury overriding my good sense.

Two of his biggest goons were guarding the entrance to his territory: Frank, an absolutely enormous orange tabby, and Gill, a sleek pure-gray tom who was freakishly big, and not in a fat way. I sucked in a deep breath and marched up to them. "Hey, I need to talk to Vinny."

Vinny was Scar's ambassador, his second-in-command. And he was generally more reasonable than the devil himself. So I'd try getting somewhere with him first.

After we'd embarrassed the whiskers off them a few weeks ago, I wasn't sure how receptive Scar would be to talking to me, but Frank just nodded at Gill, who bolted off to retrieve Vinny.

Vinny, a good-sized tuxedo cat, slunk out from behind a building a few minutes later, after making me wait long enough to question my sanity for being here alone. I figured if I came unaccompanied, he'd think I was going for diplomacy. I wasn't, but having him think so was a nice touch.

"If it isn't Zoe, leader of the Clown Cats," he greeted me, sitting up tall on his haunches with a smug smirk on his ugly mug.

"Look, I'm gonna make this brief," I said, choosing not to react to his kittenish insult.

"Uh-huh. I'll believe that when I see it." His tail twitched as he stared at me, Frank and Gill taking up positions on either side of him, trying to look menacing. *And doing a smashing job of it, I might add.*

"I know you're blackmailing the River Cats," I said. "You know, they're a peaceful clowder. Why are you messing with them? They didn't do anything to deserve that."

Vinny raked the claws of his right front paw against the cement and then brought them to his face to examine them, stretching them out till the moonlight caught on them, revealing their sharpness. He was obviously trying to intimidate me.

"It's not blackmail," he insisted. "It's merely offering them protection."

"Protection from what?" My patience was wearing thin with this insufferable furball.

"Oh, you know," he looked up from his claws, "being attacked by rival factions."

"You mean by you and your thugs," I shot back.

He licked his lips. "Still protection."

"Well, I suggest you leave them alone," I warned, though I hadn't really figured out what kind of threat I'd throw at him.

"Oh, do you now?" Frank and Gill chuckled behind him as Vinny stepped closer to me. "You know, Z, you're not very good at minding your own business."

I stood my ground. "Yeah, well, someone has to look out

for the defenseless clowders who are just trying to live their best lives and aren't hurting anyone in the process."

"You think you're the self-appointed guardian of the clowders?" He flashed a dark grin. "We're all super impressed, Z. Especially Scar."

He was really trying to get under my fur, but I wasn't going to fall for that.

"Leave them alone," I hissed in his face.

"Or what?"

"Or you're gonna regret it," I warned him.

I hadn't decided what the penalty would be yet, but I was gonna come up with something good.

I walked away, my head held high and my tail swishing in the humid night breeze.

Five

Time to round up the troops. I was alive and well after confronting Vinny, but I still needed to come up with some way to deter them from messing with our new friends, the River Cats. I was hoping one of my minions would be able to come up with something appropriately menacing.

But, after explaining the situation to my gathered toms and mollies: Moony, Ziti, Priss, Hank, Amber, Ice, Cool, Daisy and Sass, the only one who offered any solutions was, surprisingly, Sass.

"You know, the thing Scar fears most is being embarrassed," she shared. "You know I'm 'friends' with Vinny—" she used the term "friends" loosely, "—and he told me Scar was wrecked after the conference room incident a few weeks ago. Can we figure out another way to embarrass him?"

"I'd like to see him captured like Moony was," Ziti finally

added. "Have him end up in the animal shelter. No one will go save him, and we'll be rid of him forever."

Hmm, that was mildly impressive. "Not a bad thought, Ziti. But how? That is the question."

"We'll figure out something," Amber added. "But it's not going to be getting too friendly with the bipeds like what happened with Moony. Scar hates the bipeds and won't go anywhere near them."

"Hmm… Filing that info away for later."

That was when I noticed Daisy and Ice batting something back and forth. They weren't paying attention at all! *Grrrrrr.* "Hey, you two, did you notice we're having an official meeting over here?"

They both froze in place, and whatever they were toying with bounced with a light clang onto the concrete pad outside our bushes. From the sound, I guessed it wasn't a mouse.

"They got distracted by something shiny," Moony supplied.

"Well, what is it?" I walked over to them, the breeze ruffling my long gray fur.

"I don't know," Daisy said, "but it's pretty! Looks like a biped kinda."

"No, I think that's a mono-ped," Moony corrected, stepping closer to examine the small silver-gray piece.

"Is that a bird on its shoulder?" Sass asked as we all crowded around the figure. It was about the size of a mouse, so I understood why it caught their eye.

I snatched it up in my mouth, the metallic tang sending a chill down my spine all the way to the tip of my tail. "I'm taking it to Cat. She'll know what it is."

CATHERINE

It was the second night Kevin hadn't shown up for work. Mr. and Mrs. Forest were in the park tonight, talking to everyone in security. It meant we had to keep our heads down and noses to the grindstone. Gloria and I had barely said a word, but I did notice Jayden and Nora walking with his parents from the Magical Mushroom Restaurant to the Tree of Wishes early in our shift. Jayden and Nora were holding hands.

Before Gloria and I could empty the trash behind the Troll Tarts stand, two cats rushed up to us. It was Zoe and Amber.

Before I could talk to them, Zoe lifted a paw and said, "Castle. Gotta show you something."

"I can't tonight," I told her. "That's not on our cleaning rotation, and the big bosses are in the park tonight."

She sighed. "Fine. Amber, spit it out."

The small light-orange tabby opened her mouth and dropped something on the ground. The nearby overhead light reflected off it, revealing a three-inch pewter figurine of some sort. I bent down, my back aching and knees creaking, and brought it up to examine it, stepping into the light.

I turned to tell Zoe thank you, but she and her pal had already scampered off into the woods behind Troll Tarts, possibly heading to the Wishing Pond, where park visitors tossed coins and made wishes on the cute mermaid fountain in the middle.

"Well, what is it?" Gloria asked, joining me in the spot-light cast from the overhead streetlamp.

"It looks like a pirate figurine," I said, turning it over. "It's got a little parrot on its shoulder, look." I dropped it into her outstretched hand.

She brought it close to her eyes and squinted. "Hey, there's something carved here on the one foot." The other was a peg leg—so no foot. "It looks like initials. Is that...? I can't quite tell; my vision's not too good." She handed it back to me.

I had bifocals, and at this moment, they were saving the day. I examined the bottom of the pirate's buckle-festooned boot. Sure enough, two letters were carved into the pewter. "B.T." I ran those letters through the database of my mind. "Could it be Bree Townsend by any chance?"

Gloria's head tilted as she considered the probability it was our friend at Dragon's Lair Pizza. "Probably just a coincidence but..."

"Let's try talking to her again this morning when she comes in," I said. "Maybe without that pimply guy around, she'll be a little more forthcoming."

"Why don't we try to catch her right when she gets in the park? Before she clocks in," Gloria suggested.

"Good idea. We'll clock out a little early and go wait by the gate for her." Then we wouldn't have to worry about Tomato Guy interrupting us.

"Sounds like a plan, but for now, we better get back to work. Sheri's been in the park every night this week, and now that the Forests are here, I'm sure she's on the prowl, trying to make sure we're doing our jobs," Gloria reminded me.

"Alright, come on…" I sighed. Detective work was so much more fun than my real job.

WE WERE BOTH EXHAUSTED FROM WORKING OUR FINGERS TO the bone. Sheri greeted us when we went to clock out, and our shift manager, Karen, was with her, back from her leave of absence, apparently.

"Well, ladies, have a good night?" Sheri asked. Karen stood there, watching her new boss from the corner of her eye.

Our plans for clocking out early might have just been foiled. *Crud!*

"Yeah, just a normal night." I shrugged, the poster child for nonchalance.

"I have a doctor's appointment this morning, so I'm heading out a few minutes early," Gloria claimed as she punched her timecard in the antique system.

Oh, look at her working the system to her advantage! I flashed her a proud smile then quickly schooled my features into a more neutral expression so Sheri and Karen didn't see.

"I'm driving her to the doctor, so I gotta go too," I chimed in as I punched my own card. "See y'all later!"

We both stifled our giggles as we wearily trekked out of the facility services building. I would have felt like a school-girl if it weren't for the aching joints.

"Whew, I think we got away with it." Gloria beamed as we headed for the exit.

We were about halfway down Storybook Street when I

spotted vibrantly colored hair. "Oh, that's her!" I elbowed Gloria. "She must have come in early."

"Let's offer to buy her coffee," Gloria suggested.

"Good thinking." I waited until we were a little closer, then called out, "Oh, hi, Bree. How's it going?"

Her nose wrinkled up as she took in our haggard appearance. Well, mine, anyway. I swear Gloria always looked fresh as a daisy after a full shift. I looked like a swamp creature or something. I should be careful, or Mr. Forest might ask me to play a character in the park. Probably something that runs around scaring children in the Haunted Wood.

"Uh, hi." She kept walking.

"Can we chat for a second?" I asked as she passed us. "Please? I think we got off on the wrong foot the other day."

"We'll buy you coffee," Gloria added.

That did it. Bree whipped around, a tiny smile etched on her face. "Coffee?"

"Yeah, how does that sound?" I fished in my purse for a gift card I had to Troll Tarts bakery, which was just up Storybook Street on our right.

"Sure, fine," she said reluctantly. "But I only have a few minutes."

"If you're late, I'll tell Tony to excuse your tardiness," Gloria offered. "We go way back."

"Huh, okay." She shrugged and followed us down the middle of the cobblestone path until we came to the bakery. The façade actually looked like a giant cake with a troll doll on top, its wild hair blowing in the morning breeze. They were famous for their troll tarts, which were kind of like homemade Pop-Tarts but way better, and they came in all sorts of flavors: trollberry, apple cinnamon, pumpkin spice, chocolate, and s'mores.

We all ordered coffee then went to sit at a little table by the front window. It was still early in the morning, so no guests were in the park, but some of the eateries opened early so employees could stop in for a bite before or after our shifts. I stirred some sweetener into my coffee and took a sip. It was still scalding hot.

"Okay, so we want to talk about Kevin," I started off our conversation, "but we don't want to upset you."

"It's fine. Nathan was just being extra," she said. "He has been giving me a hard time about Kevin all summer, even since before we went out."

"Oh, Nathan is Tomato Guy?" I clarified.

"The guy I was working with, yes. He has a crush on me, I think. He's only seventeen." She rolled her eyes. "I'm twenty-two, so obvs he's totally cringe."

"Got it," I said. "Now, he said Kevin played something-or-other at a local game shop…"

Bree finished her sip of coffee and set her cup on the table. "Yeah, it's The Wizard's Spell in downtown Charleston. His uncle owns it. Kevin is a totally different person at P 'n P than he is here at work."

"And P 'n P is the Pirates and—" I couldn't remember what it stood for now. *I'm gonna have to get one of those little yellow legal pads like Detective What's-Her-Name carries.*

"Prisons & Pirates," she filled in the blank. "It's a tabletop role-playing game, kind of like Dungeons & Dragons, but it takes place on the sea. You're on a ship led by a captain, and you have to complete different quests on various islands. Kevin is an SC…a Ship Captain."

I was starting to think the figurine Zoe brought me had something to do with this game.

"He doesn't go by Kevin at the shop," she shared.

"No? What does he go by?" I felt like we were finally getting somewhere.

"He goes by The Silver Dagger," she said.

"How long did you guys date?" Gloria asked.

"Oh, just since June. So, what, like two months?"

"Is it true he broke up with you?" I questioned.

She hung her head for a moment, staring at the table. Then she looked up, but it wasn't sadness in her eyes. It was rage. "Yeah, he dumped me for one of the girls on his ship. Cassidy."

She said the name like it was the vilest word in the entire language, like it was poison on her tongue. It was clear the entire situation disgusted her.

"I'm sorry to hear that." Gloria reached out and patted the young woman's hand.

"It's…whatever, you know? But she's like nineteen. She's practically a kid. He's twenty-four." She rolled her eyes. "Men are so dumb."

I couldn't disagree with her assessment. My ex-husband was certainly no prize.

"Do you think his disappearance has anything to do with Cassidy?" I probed a little deeper.

She shrugged. "I mean, I don't know why she would want him to disappear. They seemed pretty happy together. Disgustingly so, in fact."

"So, his game is on Thursday nights?" I queried, patting the figurine in my pocket. Tomorrow was Thursday.

"Yeah, but I quit after he dumped me."

I pulled out the tiny pewter pirate and laid it on the table. "Know anything about this?"

"Oh!" she shrieked, picking it up. "This is mine. It was stolen from me."

"At the game store?"

"Probably." She shrugged again and stuffed the piece in her purse. *Guess we aren't getting that back.*

"So the BT on the boot is for Bree Townsend?" Gloria asked.

"Yeah. Kevin gave me the piece when we first started dating," she explained. "He bought it for me at the shop. His uncle gives him a discount."

"I see. Well, this information really helps." I braved another sip of my coffee, finding it was finally cool enough to enjoy.

She leaned forward, light blue eyes bouncing between both of us. "Why do you guys care, anyway?"

Gloria smiled. "We're concerned about him, of course. Everyone in the park is. The Forests were here last night asking around about him. They don't want to see the park shut down again over another employee, you know?"

She sighed. "Oh, yeah, that. Well, it happened right around the time he dumped me, so I wasn't really paying attention. I woulda called out sick if we hadn't been closed. I didn't wanna see him for a few days."

"That's understandable." I stood up, and Gloria followed. I hoped we didn't run into Sheri or Karen, or they'd know we didn't skedaddle out of here for a doctor's appointment. "Well, thank you for speaking with us, and if you think of anything else pertinent, can you let me know? I can give you my number?"

"Yeah, okay," she conceded.

I fished a pen from my purse and scrawled my cell phone number on a napkin. "Thanks again, Bree."

She shrugged, grabbed her coffee cup and was out the door without so much as a thank you for the coffee.

"Pleasant young lady." Gloria tsked, shaking her head.

"We have to go to that game shop, find out more about Cassidy. Talk to his uncle."

Gloria sighed as we made our way out the door. "I had a feeling you were going to say that."

I smiled. "Don't worry. I have a plan."

Six

We needed a night off—because we had work to do.

Outside the park.

But I couldn't just call out sick and get the job done myself. It was going to take some coordination and cooperation on my part, and though I was often a bit snarky and abrasive, I could be diplomatic when I needed to be.

First step: talking to Jayden.

"Hey, have you seen Jayden or Nora?" I asked Gloria as she wrung out her mop. She'd started work without me tonight. I'd forgive her for that if she didn't ask me too many questions about why I was late.

She shook her head and pinned her chocolate-brown eyes on me. "Uh oh. I see that look. What are you planning now?"

Couldn't get a darn thing past her.

I sighed and filled her in, watching her eyes growing

wider by the minute. "Well, bless your heart, dumplin'," she dismissed me with a wave of her hand. "I do believe I'm gonna sit this one out. But I hope y'all find what y'all looking for."

Before I could say another word, Jayden, Nora and a couple other young'uns who were seasonal workers came around the bend with buckets and those grabber tools you use to pick up trash. My eyes lit up as I saw Jayden direct his crew to their next task. He was turning out to be a good leader. His parents would be so proud.

"Hey, Jay, can I talk to you for a sec?" I gestured him over with a curled finger.

"Sure thing, Cat, what's up?" He headed toward us, Nora right on his heels. Apparently these two were a package deal now.

I looked him up and down. "I need your help—and your father's."

His dark eyebrow quirked. "What do you mean?"

I let them in on my plan, and he nodded. "Dad's still in his office. Let's go ask. You do the talking though. He's more likely to say yes to you."

I chuckled and shot Gloria a wink. She was scrubbing down a bench that someone had spilled ice cream on. *Yuck.* "Good luck, y'all," she gave us her blessing.

We headed to the front of the park. Mr. and Mrs. Forest had two offices: one in the Guest Services building at the entrance, and one at the very top of the tree where they could look out across their whole kingdom. We took the elevator to the top floor of the Guest Services building and stepped out, our shoes squeaking on the shiny tile echoing down the corridor as we approached the executive suite at the end.

Jayden didn't knock, just twisted the handle and swung the door open. "Hey, Pop. D'ya remember Cat from Facility Services who helped with the Heather Suka case?"

James Forest, a short, stocky man, stood up from behind his desk with an outstretched hand. I reached for him, and we made contact. He pumped my arm up and down rather vigorously before breaking contact. Then he gestured toward one of the leather chairs across from him. "Of course I remember Ms. Catherine Lyon. You're a hero around here!"

"Well, I had help," I admitted as I settled in the chair.

Jayden offered the other chair to Nora and stood behind her as his father sat down again in the biggest, fanciest executive chair I'd ever seen before. His office was a rather traditional, manly space. Tall mahogany bookshelves lined the walls, filled with books, binders and tons of nicely framed family photos. Multiple generations of the Forest family were featured in the park, on boats, in downtown Charleston, at one of the local plantations, at weddings, at graduations. It was a family history displayed right here in the park founder's office.

Mr. Forest folded his dimpled hands together and leaned toward us. "What can I do for you, Catherine?"

"So...I'm assuming Kevin Morris is still missing?" I began.

His brows immediately furrowed. "Unfortunately. I have the police working on it, but they haven't turned up anything yet. They said Kevin is a loner... That's pretty much all I got out of his immediate supervisor and coworkers as well."

"Right, well, I'm doing some digging of my own," I

shared. "And I have some ideas, but to pursue this further, I need a big favor."

His bushy eyebrows arched. "What can I do for you? You're one of my favorite employees, you know."

This man had no idea who I was until I helped solve Heather Suka's murder, but it was nice to have some recognition now. Never mind that I'd been here for twenty-plus years. Solving murders was apparently more valuable than cleaning restrooms.

More fun too, I had to admit.

"I know you'd like to avoid the press picking up this story, so I think investigating in-house makes a lot of sense," I continued. "I've been talking to some other employees who knew Kevin, and they've told me about his alter ego."

"Alter ego?" Now Mr. Forest's curiosity was piqued. There was a twinkle in his eyes.

"Yes. Apparently he goes by the name of Silver Dagger at a game store in downtown Charleston, which is owned by his uncle. He is the head honcho of some board game they play on Thursday nights…"

"And tomorrow night is Thursday." Mr. Forest already seemed to be following me.

"Yes! I called the store earlier today to ask if the game was still on tomorrow, and they told me they are starting a new one since their ship captain—that's what the game's leader is called—has mysteriously vanished. So I thought we'd check it out, see if we can talk to some of his friends and get any ideas about what happened to him."

"Oh, well, you can certainly have the night off to do that." He laced his fingers together and grinned as if he'd just given me a golden ticket to Willy Wonka's chocolate factory.

"Right, well...I don't think a fifty-something-year-old woman would be very believable as a new player to the game, which is called Prisons & Pirates, by the way—"

"So she wants me to do it," Jayden interjected. "Me and Nora."

"I see. So you're all asking for the night off," he said, seeming a little more hesitant now.

"Yes," I confirmed. "Park attendance is slowing down now that the season is coming to an end and school is about to start back up. We still have the temp workers though, so we're actually a bit overstaffed in Facility Services right now."

As soon as I said it, I regretted it. You should never tell your boss you're overstaffed. DUH! Oh, well, it had to be done. If something bad happened to Kevin Morris, and it was related to the park in any way, they might have to shut down again, and then I'd have no job at all. The entire park might be unstaffed in a matter of days if we didn't find this guy and get back to business as usual.

"Okay. No problem," Mr. Forest said, nodding and jotting down a note on his desk calendar. "Consider the night off granted. But I want a full report of what you've discovered on Friday."

"No problem," I agreed. "Thank you so much, Mr. Forest."

"Now, now, Cat," he said, shaking his head, "I'm quite sure I've asked you to call me James."

"Right, James, sorry. We'll do our very best."

"Excellent!" He shook my hand again, and then we were off to do our dirty jobs.

ZOE

Summer was drawing to a close. The sun was sinking into the trees earlier and earlier each night. As a cat, I didn't have any tools like the bipeds to help me keep track the passing of time. From what I understood of biped culture, they were obsessed with time. They used things like watches, phones, clocks, calendars, and some big colorful ball dropping on something called New Year's Eve to help them track it. We felines didn't worry about all that. We had the sun, moon and stars to guide us, and that was good enough for me.

I was feeling rather introspective tonight, and just before park closing, I slunk, unnoticed, across the center courtyard and into the trees along the river where the Water Fairy Adventure ride carried passengers on small wooden boats with fairy figureheads on the front. They went through a show building and then down a small flume before circling on a track down the river and returning to the loading dock.

I'd always wondered what the ride looked like inside, what it felt like to ride one of those boats. I hid in the reeds and watched a boat with a mermaid fairy, complete with tails and wings—*how did bipeds come up with this stuff, anyway?*—slide up the ramp to the loading dock, jerking to a stop.

"Pretty cool, huh?" came a deep, vibrating voice from somewhere else in the marsh.

As soon as I heard the voice, I caught a whiff of a male

cat, and the hair along my spine and tail prickled. I held my breath as a large white tom came into view. I'd never seen him before.

He perched on the bank of the river next to me, his tail curling around him. It was ringed, like a raccoon, contrasting with his short pure-white fur.

"Who are you?" we both asked at the same time.

I straightened my spine, lifting my chin and letting the cooler evening breeze ruffle the fur along my neck. "I'm Zoe, leader of the Courtyard Clowder. And you are?"

"I'm Snow, of course." He lifted his paw and gestured down his chest.

"Of course."

Snow, huh? Sounds like he would fit right in with Ice and Cool.

"Well, Snowman is my full name. But most cats call me Snow," he continued.

"What clowder are you part of? I've never seen you before." I looked him up and down. If he was a spy sent by Scar…

"Oh, I'm new here. Currently unaffiliated."

"Is that so?" I looked him over. His smell was intoxicating, a mixture of adventure and danger—two of my favorite things.

"That is so." He had a confident swagger that intrigued me. I almost didn't know whether to knock him down a few pegs or drop everything and follow him into the sunset.

We both sat there, the wind rustling the tall cattails around us. Clouds had rolled in and muted the sunset colors. Everything was turning gray, and the bipeds in the boats coming down the river were huddled together.

"Did you notice that boat?" Snow seemed unfazed by the approaching storm.

I stared at the boat heading our way, and a smile lit my face. "It's a cat fairy!"

"Yeah, first thing I noticed when I snuck in here."

"Wait, what?" My head whipped toward him.

"First thing I noticed when I snuck in here," he clarified.

"Yeah, I heard you the first time, but what do you mean, you snuck in here?"

"I came on the river," he said matter-of-factly.

"You what? How did you do that?"

"There's no fence over the river," he explained, "so I floated right in."

"Floated right in on *what*?" My feline brain was having a hard time picturing a cat voluntarily floating down a river.

"On a piece of wood. Our boat capsized."

"Capsized?" I didn't know that word.

"Yeah, it flipped over. It was every cat for himself." He was so nonchalant, like completely unfazed by any of it.

"There were other cats on the boat?"

"No. Just me. But there were some bipeds. 'Every cat for himself' is just a saying, okay?"

"What happened to them?" I asked. "The bipeds?"

"I don't know. They were fighting. That's why we capsized." He yawned. Either recounting this tale was tiring, or he was just bored.

I was completely captivated by this story. I had no idea there was a way to sneak onto park property, or that the river was perhaps an escape to freedom. I filed that information away for later. I wasn't a big fan of water, but...

"Was one of the bipeds your owner?" I asked.

"Owner?" he scoffed. "No, I prefer to think of him as my subordinate."

"I see." Well, that did make sense. We were cats, after all. Could we really be "owned"? "So you just floated right into the park?"

"Yeah, that's right. Noticed there were some lovely females in the area, so thought I'd stick around for a while." He licked his lips as he stared at me.

Is he flirting with me?

"You don't think your biped is looking for you?"

Snow gave the tiniest shrug. "Not too concerned about him, really."

I wanted to ask him even more questions, but right then, lightning streaked across the sky, and thunder rumbled just after. One more clap of thunder, and the rain began to pour, soaking my fur in record time. I hated being wet. Hated it. I didn't know how the River Cats could stand it.

"C'mon, I know a place to hide," Snow said.

And before I knew it, I was following him to shelter.

I was following *him*.

Ugh!

Seven

CATHERINE

It wasn't quite night yet at The Wizard's Spell game shop we were infiltrating for their Thursday game night. Apparently, they had four different games going on, and I coached Jayden and Nora on which table they were to join. I found parking only a block away and headed to the shop as the wind kicked up around me. A storm was blowing in, and the palms were waving wildly as dusk blanketed the peninsula.

I was planning to arrive after Jayden and Nora got settled in so it didn't look suspicious. In my research about the shop, I learned Steve Morris was the owner—I assumed that was Kevin's uncle. I was going to come in, do some shopping, pretend to be very interested in one of the other games going on and see if I could eavesdrop on any of the conversations at the Prisons & Pirates table. Then I was going to hang out in the coffee shop next door until Jayden and Nora could join me.

Ah, it was good to have a plan. I just hoped it didn't all fall apart.

The shop had a musty smell that was covered up with incense so strong, it nearly made me gag—and I was used to some pretty unsavory smells thanks to my job and being a boy mom. Yeah, my sons were grown up now, but you just didn't forget some of those odors, you know? There was also a constant hum of chatter punctuated by occasional raucous laughter as I perused the shelves.

I spotted my comrades at the table, learning the game as they interacted with the seven other people in attendance. The young man at the head of the eight-foot table had long dyed-black hair, vividly pale skin, and dark eyes rimmed in eyeliner. I was pretty sure that look, in combination with his dark clothing accented by various chains and other hardware, was called "goth," but I didn't want to use the wrong label.

I headed over to a case of puzzles nearby as I attempted to listen in.

"If you roll a seventeen, then you can invoke the sea dragon spell," the young woman next to Jayden explained. She wore her honey-blond hair in a messy bun piled on top of her head. Unlike the dude in black, she had sun-kissed skin and wore nothing but a pink gingham crop top adorned with embroidered strawberries and a tiny pair of denim shorts with pink eyelet trim. She had a unicorn tattoo on her ankle and her toenails were painted glittery pink.

"Cassidy, I'll explain the rules," the man at the head of the table scolded her.

"Sorry, Ship Captain Drago." She looked down at the figurine in her hands forlornly.

Nora and Jayden exchanged a look, and Jayden spoke up, "I heard you had to start a new game because your previous ship captain disappeared."

Oh, way to cut to the chase, Jayden, I silently praised him. Of course, I continued to mind my own business, picking up various puzzles to examine before returning them to the shelf. Then I moved on to the next case that held board games the likes of which I'd never seen before. I had no idea there were so many games beyond the standards like *Monopoly, Risk,* and *Clue.*

"Not my ship captain," the leader nearly sneered. "There was another game prior to this one, and, yes, it was led by someone else."

"Was his name Kevin?" Jayden interjected. Nora reached down and squeezed his hand—maybe she thought he was pushing too hard. I had a feeling he was doing it for my benefit, knowing I was listening in.

"Kevin?" The girl with the messy bun scoffed. "No one called him that. What are you, his mom?"

Everyone around the table laughed, but I picked up on the past tense. Did "Cassidy" know something we didn't?

Then I put two and two together. This was the girl he had dumped Bree for. She was...not the type of girl I imagined would go for a guy like Kevin, at least not from what I knew of him. She was very girly and cute. Perhaps it was just infatuation with someone older than her? I wasn't sure. I just couldn't picture them together. I pictured him more with someone like Bree, someone with nerdy vibes like him.

Was that awful for me to think?

Regardless, I did feel bad about pegging them like that, and about labeling the cantankerous leader as a goth, but wasn't this what police and detectives did? They profiled people, put them into neat boxes and then used those boxes to help determine their motives and their M.O.s. That was what I was doing too, right?

Everything I knew about psychology and sociology rushed back to me as I attempted to put the puzzle pieces together. When I worked on the Heather Suka case, it was easy to figure out why someone might want to off her. She was wildly unpopular, had a lot of enemies. It was harder to narrow down the pool of potential suspects who might have been pushed over the edge to act out on their hatred toward her.

But Kevin seemed like a fairly lowkey guy. I couldn't imagine anyone hating him enough to want to hurt him. The cats didn't like him, but none of the humans I'd spoken to had an issue with him.

"Have you been playing this game for long?" Jayden continued interviewing Ship Captain Drago.

He lifted his dark eyes toward Jayden and smirked. "Do you want to go out on a date or something?"

"Oh, no, I—"

"Well, then shut up and learn the game. You're here to play, not flirt with me," he snarled.

"Sorry, Ship Captain," Jayden said.

Oops. Guess he did push a little too hard.

"Good evening, may I help you?" a deep voice came from behind me.

My heart rate took off like a spooked horse as I slowly turned around. "Um, hi, I'm just looking, thanks."

The man speaking to me had a medium build and height. He looked about my age, with a shaved head to disguise his receding hairline and intriguing green eyes. "Looking for anything in particular?"

He wore a black polo shirt with the store's logo on it. *Oh, okay, he works here. He's not some random dude trying to strike up a conversation with me.*

When I was younger, I might have been disappointed by that. But now, at fifty-five, it was a relief.

"Um…looking for a birthday present for my son," I lied, though I did have two sons, and they did have birthdays. They might actually dig this place, so maybe it could be the truth after all.

"He's into tabletop games?" the man pressed.

"Oh, um, I don't know… He's in his mid-twenties. He's a software engineer. I feel like he might enjoy something like this." I pointed to one of the games.

"Yes, that's a popular game, very broad appeal. Our games are twenty percent off right now." He grinned and rocked forward on his feet toward me, then back again. He wore fancy brand-new sneakers, a brand I'd never heard of before.

"Oh, okay. Well, I'll consider it, thank you." I just wanted to get rid of him so I could get back to eavesdropping.

"No problem. I'm Steve, if you have any questions." He turned to walk away, and I stared at his retreating back.

Oh, Steve! That must be Kevin's uncle.

I scrambled for a way to ask him questions about his nephew's disappearance. I'd figure something out. Meanwhile, I tuned back into the conversation happening at the table. They were taking a snack break, and Jayden was trying to engage Cassidy.

"Have you been playing long?" he asked.

She shrugged. "Not really. My cousin Steve got me into it. I was playing in the last voyage, the one that got disbanded because The Silver Dagger disappeared."

"Oh, really? So that guy is actually missing then?" he encouraged her to speak. "Did you know him?"

She sighed. "Yeah, we went out a couple times."

"Oh, I'm so sorry," Nora chimed in. "You must be so sad and scared for him."

She glanced down at her phone and didn't look up as she answered, "Eh. I'm sure he's fine and will turn up sooner or later."

She did not sound very torn up about it at all. Could she be involved in his disappearance? What she said about him turning up didn't match her use of past tense earlier...

I discreetly flashed a thumbs-up at Jayden and Nora as I took the game up to the counter. I was going to buy the darn thing so I had another opportunity to talk to Steve.

"It's so nice you let the young people play games here in the store." I set the game down on the counter. "Young people don't have enough places to hang out."

Steve stepped away from his computer, where he was clearly playing solitaire, and nodded. "Yeah, I feel it provides a great service to the community. And it tends to create loyal customers." He grabbed the game and aimed his scanner at the barcode. "Glad to see you chose this game. I think your son will like it."

"Thanks, I hope so too." I inserted my debit card in the reader. "I overheard the kids at the pirates table talking about having to start a new game because the last one's leader was missing. That sounds awful—did you know him?"

Steve sighed as my receipt printed. "Yeah, the missing man is actually my nephew. Fortunately, my son, Stevie, the one leading the game over there, was able to take over the table. He's been hoping for an opportunity to be the ship captain. My nephew always drew in customers, so I told Stevie he had to wait for Kev to sit out a rotation."

"Oh, really? Huh. I hope your nephew turns up soon," I said as Steve stuffed my game and receipt into a bag.

"Yeah, me too. He's a good kid. Has a good job. Very responsible. My brother and his wife are just beside themselves with worry." Steve sighed and shook his head.

"I'll be praying for your family," was all I said before stepping out into the drizzly night. From the debris in the street, I could tell it had rained heavily while I was inside.

Could Stevie the Goth Ship Captain and/or Cassidy have something to do with Kevin's disappearance?

THE STORM STARTED UP AGAIN WHILE WE WERE SAFELY ensconced in the coffee shop next door. I sipped regular coffee, knowing I wasn't going to be able to sleep anyway. I'd been on night shift for so long, sleeping at night was foreign to me. Jayden and Nora shared a chai tea latte, all cuddled up into the corner booth as we prepared our report to his father when we arrived back at the park for our shift tomorrow evening.

"Cassidy was definitely in on it," Jayden said. "She looked guilty to me. And supposedly she was dating him. She acted like she hardly knew him!"

"What did you make of her saying her cousin Steve got her into P 'n P?" I asked as I jotted notes down on the little pad I had stuffed in my purse when I was walking out the door—taking a page out of Detective Towers' book, literally.

"Stevie was the ship captain," Nora apparently felt comfortable enough to join the conversation. Good for her! Jayden was really helping her come out of her shell.

"Yes, that confirms my suspicions!" I exclaimed, but my sudden loudness caused Nora to shrink back like a scared turtle. "I spoke to Uncle Steve when I bought this game." I pointed to my paper bag with the store logo on it. "He told me his son wanted to be ship captain, but Kevin brought a lot of folks into the store on game night. Steve told his son he could be the ship captain when Kevin decided to take a break."

Jayden's entire face was animated. "Ah, interesting, so 'Stevie'—by the way, that nickname is so funny! Did you see how authoritarian the dude was?"

"Yeah," I agreed, "you could say he runs a tight ship!"

Jayden and Nora both blinked at each other, apparently not finding my pun as hilarious as it definitely was. "Runs a tight ship? C'mon, y'all, that was funny."

"Sure, Cat," Jayden agreed, and Nora just giggled.

"Do you think Stevie wanted to be ship captain so bad, he figured out a way to keep Kevin from showing up? To make him disappear?" I posited.

"Surely he wouldn't actually hurt him, right?" Jayden's brows furrowed. "I mean, they're cousins."

"You never had a cousin you were super competitive with?" Nora's small voice piped up.

We both swung our heads in her direction. "Um…no? My cousins and I are all close. We're good friends," Jayden answered.

I raised my hands, palms out. "I was never close with my cousins. They all live up north. They're Yankees."

"Well, I had a cousin about my age," Nora began, her

voice gradually gaining a little volume, "and we hated each other. We were both in line to be valedictorian of our class."

That was more words than I'd ever heard her string together at one time.

"Oh, yeah?" Jayden took her hand in his and squeezed. "And how did that turn out?"

The smuggest smile crept over Nora's face. "Well, I had a perfect four point oh. Jessica, on the other hand, barely passed calculus our senior year."

Jayden's smile glowed with pride. "That's my girl."

"Okay, back to the case," I redirected the two young'uns.

"So, what's next?" Jayden asked.

"We need to find out more about Stevie and Cassidy," I said. "I just have to figure out how to do it."

Eight

ZOE

Snow and I waited out the storm in the small outbuilding behind the Water Fairy Adventure ride. I had never been in this small building before and had no idea there was even a way to get inside, but Snow figured it out fast. He was really smart.

Once the rain let up, it was nearly time for the park to close, and the crowds were dwindling. "Wanna go on one of the last boats?" he offered.

"What? How would we do that?" I asked. "We can't let any of the bipeds see us."

"They have to run empty boats until the ones with people on them come back onto the dock," he explained. "I've been here a while now, so I've watched them close up for the night a couple of times. We can sneak on board."

"You think so?"

"Oh, yeah, for sure. Follow me!" He confidently strutted

toward the building, right where a line of bipeds extended out the doors.

"Wait!" I hissed. Clearly this guy didn't understand how important it was for us not to be seen. Plus, he was stark white! Kind of hard to miss him. At least with my gray fur, I could blend in a little easier. Still, I followed him because he was cute and smart, and I had always wanted to go on one of these boats—as long as it didn't involve getting wet.

Somehow, we slipped in right as they roped off the line, and the biped employees were so concerned with getting everyone ushered through, they didn't even notice us. My heart was racing as we stayed behind the cluster of bipeds moving toward the dock, darting between shadows and behind the trashcans strategically placed to encourage guests not to litter.

"If we hang back here, we can try to get the cat fairy boat," Snow advised as we reached the dock. The employees were dividing the bipeds into groups of six so they could slide into the three rows of seating on the boats, two to a bench. Everyone was so focused on climbing into their boat, no one noticed us traipsing further down the line and sneaking onto the one with a glorious figurehead with fairy wings and a cat's head.

I didn't know before why bipeds thought fairies were so special, but seeing the cat fairy, I had been converted. They were magical! I think I used that biped word correctly.

"C'mon, Zoe." Snow lifted his paw and pointed. "You go first. I'm right behind you." We expertly leapt on board and hid under the bench as the boats jolted forward on the track. The last boat of bipeds was three or four ahead of us, so no one was looking in any boats past that. The remaining boats would run through the ride empty.

Next thing I knew, we were splashing down into the water. A few droplets landed on my fur, and I was not a fan of that, but I was too distracted by the twinkling lights and beautiful music to mind too much.

We both perched on top of the bench once we were in the dark so we could see the mesmerizing scenery. Bipeds were pretty weird, but they sure did know how to create a feast for the senses. I sort of gathered that the story involved a poor fairy who was trapped by an evil wizard, and the rest of the fairies banded together to rescue her. It was just lovely!

And the whole time, Snow sat beside me, equally mesmerized as colorful lights and floating fairies danced before our eyes. Then the boat came to an abrupt stop, and the lights and music—everything—shut down.

"Uh…" I looked around, my eyes adjusting to the dark. I saw Snow's begin to glow in the darkness. "Now what?"

"Oh, right. Guess we aren't going to make it back around to the dock." He hopped off the bench and ran up to the front of the boat, climbing right up the end to the figurehead.

"Well, don't tell me we're trapped here!" I tried not to panic, but I totally sounded like I was panicking.

"Don't worry. We're going to figure this out. See that ledge?" His head tilted to the left.

I could barely make out a small walkway, couldn't have been any wider than my body was long. (I'm a cat. I don't use biped measurements.) "You think we can make it?"

"Sure. We always land on our feet, right?"

"That's what we want bipeds to believe." It didn't make it true, unfortunately. I'd met some seriously uncoordinated felines in my time.

"Well, it's either that or stay in the boat till morning," he said.

Well, that didn't sound like a good plan. My clowder would probably miss me, right? They'd all been so checked out lately. Moony was reveling in Priss and Ziti's fawning all over him. Hank rarely left loaf position. Daisy was so scatter-brained, she'd never realize I was gone. Sass would probably try to take over in my absence. Ice would fight her for it. Poor Mr. Cool Cat was losing touch with reality. That left Amber. She would probably do whatever Ice or Ziti told her to do.

"Okay, let's go for it." I scampered up to the top of the figurehead where there was a tiny perch just big enough for both of us to stand. Up here, I had a better view of the situation—and, unfortunately, it looked even scarier. But I'd always been pretty nimble. Snow looked agile too.

"Let's do it together," he suggested. "Ready?"

I took a deep breath and gritted my teeth before springing off the perch, flying through the air and landing with a solid thud on the small metal walkway. Snow landed right beside me.

"We did it!" he cheered. He rubbed up against me affectionately, and a shiver raced down my spine.

This was the most excitement I'd had since we embarrassed the fur out of Scar and his thugs, and I was loving every minute of it. Who needs a clowder when you have someone like Snow?

We pranced down the walkway, following it to a ramp that led outside the building and deposited us right by the river. We followed the bank around a curve until we got to the biped bridge. The rain had left everything hazy, and the park lights reflected on the water as fireflies danced in the bushes. It was a lovely evening, and the rain had brought a cool, gentle breeze.

But we barely made it over the bridge before we heard an ear-piercing squeal.

My blood turned to ice in my veins, and Snow and I both froze in place, the fur on the backs of our necks standing on end as our eyes darted around us, looking for the source of the scream. I caught sight of a few pairs of eyes glowing from under the bridge.

The River Cats.

At least I hoped so. And I hoped Scar and his goons weren't down there harassing them.

"C'mon," I said to Snow, "it's time for you to meet some more felines of Fairytale Forest."

He puffed out his chest. "Lead the way."

We ran down the embankment to the underside of the bridge where the water swelled and splashed around big boulders placed artistically in the river's bend, forming a triangle a strong cat could use to cross the current if they so chose. I looked out over the water.

Wait. I always thought there were three rocks. I spotted four this time. *Oh, well, cats aren't known for their counting skills.*

I heard a commotion and called out, "Who's there?"

Three cats stepped out from the shadows of the bridge, their eyes huge and glowing. They looked like they'd seen a ghost—*or that's what a biped would say, anyway.*

"It's me, Zoe," I announced myself, "and this is my new friend Snow. Who goes there?"

The River Cats had their own way of communicating. They didn't use the same language that we used amongst themselves. They could speak it, but they preferred silent gesturing among their own clowder. When I'd stopped by before, only their leader spoke to me.

"Zoe? It's me, Delta," said the tortoiseshell molly I'd spoken to before. Her voice warbled with fear. "I'm with Brooke and Beck, the twins you met before."

"Is there a problem?" I asked. "Is Vinny bothering you again?"

"No...worse." She stepped toward me and then looked over her shoulder. "There's something down there in the river. Something I think you should see."

"What is it?" Snow questioned, his white fur glowing in the moonlight that had suddenly appeared from behind parting clouds.

"I'm not entirely sure...possibly a biped..."

Oh no. A flashback of finding that female biped a few weeks ago coursed through me. I swallowed hard. "Possibly?"

"Let's go check it out." Snow advanced forward, looking cocky and sure-footed. The River Cats began to follow him, so I did the same, just keeping my distance so I didn't have to be the first to—

"Oh no..." Snow froze in place when we came to what, from the river bank, had looked like another rock in the water. The current was rushing around the dark lump.

"What is it, Snow?" We all caught up to him and stopped abruptly, or we would have run right into him.

"Well...remember that subordinate I was telling you about?"

I shuddered. "Yeah?"

"Well...it's him."

CATHERINE

We were on our way to talk to Mr. Forest in his office at the top of the tree when I spotted Zoe peeking out from the edge of the bush. "Hey, Cat!" she called out at me.

I was thankful no one else could hear her—her voice sounded so loud in my head! I instantly froze, and Jayden, walking beside me, also stopped. "What's wrong?"

"I need to talk to you NOW," she said, sounding adamant.

I glanced around, trying to figure out where to go. There were still tons of people in the park. How would we rendezvous somewhere we wouldn't be spotted?

"Cat?" Nora, attached to Jayden via a very insistent handhold, looked concerned.

I couldn't exactly answer Zoe right now.

"Sorry, I just twisted my ankle," I lied, then limped forward a few steps to make it look realistic. "I better go put some ice on it. Why don't you go talk to your dad, and I'll catch up with you later? Here, you can take my notes."

"You sure you're gonna be okay?" Now Jayden shared the same concerned look as Nora.

"Yeah, yeah." I waved my hand, dismissing their worry. "I'll be fine. Just want to prop it up with ice so it doesn't swell. I have weak ankles. I do this all the time. Not my first rodeo!" I kept rambling like a complete idiot.

Jayden still looked hesitant, and Zoe was standing there

with a scowl on her face—or at least the feline version of it. I had no idea how they didn't notice her fluffy gray head poking out of the bushes. "Okay, if you're sure."

"Yep, I trust you to relay all the info to your dad. Make sure to find out if he knows Steve Morris."

"Will do." Jayden gave me a mock salute.

The happy couple sauntered across the courtyard toward the tree, and I bent down close to the bush, pretending to tie my shoe. "How do you think we're going to get away with meeting right now?" I whispered.

"Behind the Goblin Go-Karts," she fired back, "there's a huge wall of tires and the enormous goblin figures. There's nothing else back there. Meet me there. It's important."

"Okay." I rose to standing, glancing around to see if anyone was watching me. I came in early so I could talk to Mr. Forest, so I had some time to kill, but it was broad daylight. I didn't want to run into Karen or Sheri. I needed to get lost in the crowd and pretend to be a park guest right now. Which wasn't going to be easy because I was wearing my uniform.

Then I remembered I had an old t-shirt in my bag. I carried one with me in case I had a really gross job. Then I'd change and get it dirty and possibly stained instead of my uniform shirt. I slipped into one of the women's restrooms, cringing at the mess—*I'll have to clean that up later* —exchanged my shirts, and I was on my way to the go-kart track.

There wasn't anything particularly goblin-y about the go-karts. The Forests obviously just wanted to have go-karts and needed to find a fantasy theme. They loved alliterative attraction names so I was sure that was where it came from. The go-karts were painted green, and there was a tall goblin mural circling the track, complete with two giant wooden goblin figures on the back side that separated the track from the river.

I blended into the crowd as though I was going to get on the ride, then I slipped around the fence, making sure no one was watching. I darted behind the tower of tires stacked in front of the goblin cutouts and finally behind the structure, which was probably twenty feet tall. Bonus points: the go-karts were so loud, no one would hear Zoe and me talking.

She was alone—which was unusual for her. I found her pacing back and forth like a tiger in a cage. "What's wrong?"

She stopped in her tracks, stared at me for a moment, and then rushed toward me. "Oh, Cat, we have a problem. A very big problem."

"What kind of problem?" I leaned in, watching Zoe continue to pace.

"We found another body," she said, stopping long enough to face me.

"What?! Oh no!" My hands flew to my face, scrubbing down it as dread filled every cell in my body. "When? Where?"

"Last night," she said. "It's under the bridge."

"Oh no… you mean just over there?" I pointed toward the river and the Water Fairy Adventure boat ride. The boats didn't go as far as the bridge, but plenty of pedestrians crossed it to get to the ride.

"Yes."

"Is it Kevin Morris?" I asked, bracing myself for the answer.

"If Kevin also goes by The Silver Dagger, then yes."

"Oh no. Oh my gosh…I don't know what to do." I started pacing back and forth too. I couldn't exactly delay telling Mr. Forest about this tragic turn of events, but I also didn't want to draw any guests' attention to a dead body in the park! At least Heather's body was found at night when no one was around. There would be complete pandemonium if a guest discovered the body, or if they went to extract it while guests were here.

I had to think quick.

Jayden and Nora were still in his dad's office. I had to go now and tell him what was going on so he could make the decision.

"Thank you for letting me know, Zoe. I don't suppose you can tell what happened to him…?"

"No. His body is face-down in the shallows under the bridge. I think he might actually be caught on something because the water was rushing around him, and the body didn't move. He was wearing dark clothing so he kind of looked like another rock. There are some other real rocks around him."

"Right. Maybe that's why no one has noticed." I shook my head, panic surging through me. How could this be happening again?

Did Stevie Morris murder his cousin, and if so, how did his body get into the park? Did Cassidy have something to do with it? Did Bree?

I was so confused and devastated. "I have to go tell the park owner. I'll try to come find you later tonight. If you find any clues or anything at all you think might be important, please let me know, alright?"

She stared at me with her brilliant green eyes, her gray plume of a tail swaying behind her. "I will."

Before I left, she called to me, "I've lived here in Fairytale Forest almost my entire life, and nothing like this ever happened. Then two dead employees in one moon cycle? What's going on with you bipeds, Cat?"

I shook my head, fear and sadness intertwined coursing through me. "I wish I had an answer to that, Zoe."

Nine

CATHERINE

The first person I ran into when I got back over to the central area of the park was Gloria. "Have you seen Jayden?" flew out of my mouth.

"Hello to you too!" she retorted.

"Sorry, we have a bit of a situation. I need to know if Jayden is still in his dad's office at the top of the tree."

"Haven't seen him. Sorry, sugarplum." She sighed as she pulled on her gloves. "Are you coming to help me with the restrooms?"

"Sorry, I've gotta find Jayden and Mr. Forest." I waved as I practically sprinted—well, what counts for sprinting when you're a fifty-five-year-old fluffy chick with arthritis and bone spurs—toward the tree.

"I better get a full report as soon as you get back here," she called after me.

I raced to the elevator in the tree and pressed the button

for the top floor, but the elevator just stood there with the doors shut, not moving. *Darn it! You need a code to get up to the top office. I almost forgot. Crud.*

I backed out, not knowing what the code was. Security would know. And they could call up and make sure Mr. Forest was still here.

This time I headed out of the tree and around back to the Security entrance. "Is Derek in?" I sputtered.

"Well, look what the cat dragged in," came his sneer from the hallway where his office was. "Why are you here, Cat?"

"Look, I have some information, and I need to talk to Mr. Forest stat. Is he still in his office up there?" I pointed up.

"Wouldn't you like to know?" Derek taunted me.

"Listen, this is important. If you don't help me get up to Mr. Forest's office right now, you're going to regret it." I stood with my arms folded over my chest, giving him my "I mean business" look that I perfected on my sons when they were younger.

"Fine," he conceded, "but I'm coming with you."

Derek was Kevin's boss, so he might as well be in on the conversation. I followed him down the hall to Security's private elevator that I wouldn't otherwise have access to. We stepped inside, he pressed the button, and we zoomed up to the top of the tree.

When we stepped out, Jayden and Nora were leaving. "Hey, Cat, you okay?"

I suddenly remembered I was supposed to have a twisted ankle. *Oops!*

I limped toward them. "Yeah, but I need to talk to your dad right now. C'mon, you guys can come too."

"You shouldn't be walking on that ankle," he chided me as we rushed toward the executive suite at the end of the hall.

"I feel much better," I said. "I took some ibuprofen, and I'm good as new. C'mon, this is urgent."

"Dad? I'm back—Cat and Derek from Security are here now with an update," Jayden said as we all slipped through the door he was holding.

James Forest was dressed down today in khaki pants and a green polo shirt with the Fairytale Forest logo on it. "What's going on? Cat, did you find Kevin?"

"Everyone, sit down." I gestured to the sofas in the atrium area of his office. It was beautiful with skylights overhead that showed golden clouds moving through azure skies as the sun began its nightly descent.

"Tell me what's going on," Mr. Forest demanded. "Does this have to do with Kevin?"

"I just found out Kevin's body has been discovered in the park," I rushed out.

"What? Where? Discovered by who?" our boss demanded.

"It's under the bridge over the river, near Water Fairy Adventure. You know, the pedestrian bridge? I came straight here as soon as I found out because I didn't want to create a scene, or for any guests to see it."

"Did you see it with your own eyes? How did you know it was him?" Derek asked before Mr. Forest could say anything.

"The cats told me," I blurted out.

Then I froze.

Um.

Oops. I wasn't supposed to say that.

"The cats did what?!" Jayden was the first to process what I accidentally said.

"Um, sorry, I mean I saw some cats hanging around down there. Aren't there three big boulders in the river near the bridge?" I looked around at everyone's faces to gauge the answer.

"Yes, three," Mr. Forest confirmed. "That was my wife's idea. They represent the Holy Trinity."

Um, okay.

"Well, it looks like there are four rocks right now."

"Holy Mother of Gobstoppers!" Mr. Forest exclaimed.

That was a creative swear, but, yeah.

"So what should we do?" I glanced around the room again.

"Sir, I highly suggest waiting until park closing. We'll call the police and get the coroner out here to move the body."

Mr. Forest looked at his watch. "Three more hours till closing. Hopefully no one will notice."

Derek stood up. "I'll call Facility Services and get them to take the orange construction fence over there. Guests will just think we're refurbishing the bridge or adding a new attraction."

Mr. Forest's face lit up. "It will start rumors—but they'll be positive ones. And it will distract everyone for the time being. Good thinking, Derek." Then he turned to me. "Once again, Cat, you're the one to find the body."

I didn't want to correct him.

But I also didn't want to be known as the employee who always found the dead bodies.

I never wanted any notoriety at all in this job. I simply wanted to empty trash and clean bathrooms, and that would be the end of it.

I certainly didn't want this.

"We've got to keep this on the downlow," Mr. Forest said in a low voice, as if someone would overhear our conversation and the rumor mill would explode like fireworks. "We must do a better job than we did in the Heather Suka case. There is still a good chance there's no foul play at all—that Kevin just disappeared and met an untimely demise. Let's think positive thoughts until we get a cause of death. And, in the meantime, protect the park from the word getting out at all costs."

"At all costs," we all repeated.

ZOE

I knew Cat had relayed the message about the biped body when the park closed and a swarm of bipeds in uniforms descended upon the bridge over the river. It took several bipeds to pull the body out of the current. In the process, the poor deceased biped's shirt was ripped off after getting caught on something in the river.

An interesting mark stood out on the pale, grayish skin as they carried him to a stretcher. I wasn't sure what it was, or if I could describe it to Cat. It looked like something sharp—a knife or weapon of some sort? And on the handle was an eerie-looking oval shape with dark patches that seemed to make up a face, and under that were two bones that crossed each other.

What was becoming of this park we called home? Guests

had always visited and seemed happy, seemed to be having fun. Now it was becoming a place of death, at least in the dark.

When we found the last dead biped, Cat worried they would close down the park. No guests equaled no food, which equaled no mice or meals for felines. What would become of all of us if the park shut down? Would they round us up and take us to the shelter like what happened to my brother when Scar targeted him?

Would we all be separated?

Once again, I needed to help Cat and her friends solve this mystery so life as we knew it could continue.

As they carried the body back to the waiting ambulance —I knew of the vehicle from TV shows I used to watch with the Security bipeds—I realized I was not alone. Snow had sidled up next to me. He'd always had plenty to say, but now he was silent.

"So that was your biped?" I asked.

He stared unseeing at the flashing lights as they drove down the service road and out the side gates of the park. He didn't answer me.

When I met him, he was so full of life and confident nearly to the brink of cockiness. And now he was just a shell as he watched the biped who had fed and sheltered him his whole life be carried out into the big beyond.

This is why I shouldn't get attached to Cat or any other bipeds, I reminded myself. No matter how closely I had to work with them to solve the mystery, I couldn't get attached.

I wouldn't set myself up for the heartbreak of losing a special biped.

It was bad enough we were on the verge of losing Mr. Cool Cat.

I sucked in a deep breath, filling my lungs with the warm night air that carried the slightest hint of brine. I refused to get emotional. I was a cat, darn it, and being aloof and unattached was a distinctly feline art form.

An art form I would master.

Ten

Gloria and I headed over to the Princess and the Pea Castle, our usual meeting place with Zoe, on our break. We took snacks. I hoped to see her on the way since we were walking through the courtyard, but I didn't. The police and medical examiner were in the park—I saw the flashing red and blue lights as the vehicles entered the north gate and traveled toward the river on the service roads.

"I can't believe he's dead," Gloria said sadly, looking down at her bag of pretzels. "I don't even know if I can eat this."

"We have to keep up our strength. We'll need to get our work done while also investigating what happened," I reminded her before popping a Cheeto into my mouth.

"It surely isn't another murder though." Gloria ripped open the bag of pretzels and slowly lifted one to her mouth.

Then she chewed thoughtfully as I thought about her statement.

"Well, you know what? I feel like murder is more believable than him ending up in that river by accident. He was a fit young man. And if he didn't know how to swim, why would he have gone near the water? We know he was here in the morning when we left, and then he left right after we did. I guess the real question is what happened between then and when he ended up in the water?"

"So you don't think he drowned?" Gloria questioned.

I shook my head. "Why would he be in the river if he couldn't swim? It just makes no sense to me."

I was still pondering what might have happened to him when I heard a commotion. I looked up to find Zoe bounding into the castle's atrium with a white cat with a ringed tail on her heels. I hadn't seen this one before. He was gorgeous and definitely didn't look like a stray—nor a cat who could easily stay hidden.

"Hey, we were just talking about you," I told her.

She sat up on her haunches and looked me over, then she turned to her companion. "Snow, this is Cat and Gloria, the bipeds I was telling you about."

"Hi, Snow," I greeted him. "Nice to meet you."

He just stared at me silently, his blue eyes wide and observant.

"He's a handsome boy," I told Zoe. "I assume he can't understand me?"

"No. But listen—this male biped found in the river?"

"Yes, it's Kevin Morris," I confirmed. "I gave the information to the park owner, and he called the police. They're here now."

"Yes," Zoe confirmed. "We just watched them remove the body. Snow lived with Kevin."

I stared at the handsome white feline next to Zoe. "Wait, that's Kevin's cat?"

"Well, we don't really subscribe to the whole ownership thing, but he did live in Kevin's apartment," Zoe explained.

"How did—" I shook my head as Gloria finally put together my side of the conversation since she couldn't hear Zoe.

"This cat was Kevin's?" She pointed to Snow. "How did he get in the park?"

"That's what I want to know." We both faced Zoe, waiting for the answers.

"Snow said that he and Kevin were on a boat with some other bipeds, and there was a fight. The boat capsized. Snow was able to float on a small piece of wood that broke off the boat, and the current carried him down the river and into the park. There's no fence over the river."

"That's right. What a terrible idea for park security," I groaned.

Mr. Forest had been too cheap to build a barrier over the river, or maybe the environmental folks wouldn't let him. I wasn't sure what the actual park boundary looked like at the river. Could they really just float down and into the park? Surely there was some sort of barrier there...

"What happened to the other bipeds?" I asked Zoe.

She asked Snow the question, and I did not hear his reply. I still didn't understand why Zoe and I could understand each other, but no other humans could hear her, and I couldn't hear any other cats. It was just this connection between the two of us. Where did it come from? How was it possible?

I still hadn't totally dismissed the idea that I was going crazy, but Gloria was right here watching me have what, to her, appeared to be a one-sided conversation, and she apparently didn't think I'd totally lost it.

"He doesn't know," she finally answered. "He barely got himself on top of the board, and then he floated away. He never saw Kevin or the other bipeds."

"How many were there?" I followed up.

She asked him and returned, "He's not sure. He said he never really paid attention to Kevin and his friends because they were wildly boring. They only cared about some stupid game they played that was something about pirates. Whatever those are."

"Oh, yeah, pirates—that might not be a familiar concept to you." I turned to Gloria and explained, "Prisons & Pirates is what they play at the game shop in Charleston."

"Didn't you say his cousin took his spot in the game?" Gloria asked.

"Yes. So we wondered if Stevie had anything to do with Kevin's disappearance." I asked Zoe, "He wouldn't know if one of the humans—I mean bipeds—was named Stevie, would he?"

She asked him and turned back to me, her tail twitching. "He doesn't know any of their names."

I let out a breathy sigh. "Well, that tells us a little bit, but not nearly enough."

Gloria folded her bag of pretzels and slid it into her purse. "Well, even if he *was* able to identify all the people on board that boat, what would we do, go to the police and say, 'Hey, a cat identified these guys as suspects'? They would never believe us."

"Good point. We'll have to figure out another way," I agreed. "I wonder what happened to the boat."

"Sounds like we'll need to go figure out where the river exits the park," Gloria said. "Look for clues."

It sounded like she was starting to get interested in this case, much like Jayden and Nora were. Between all of us, surely we could put the pieces together. We had to, for Kevin's sake. For the park's sake.

"Oh, I did notice something that may or may not be relevant when they lifted the body out of the water," Zoe said.

"Oh, yeah? What's that?" I asked while Gloria waited to hear the translation.

"The biped's shirt was caught on something in the water," Zoe explained. "Maybe that is why he drowned; I don't know. In any case, it came off when they moved him, and he had a picture on his fur."

"Oh, a tattoo?" I clarified. Gloria's eyes widened. "On his skin?"

"Yes. I guess that's what you bipeds call it. I have seen the pictures before, but not one so big." She spread her front paws together to indicate about twelve inches.

"What was it? Where was it on his body?" I asked, then turned to Gloria. "She noticed he had a tattoo."

Gloria nodded.

"It was on his back and looked like a knife or some sort of weapon." Zoe struggled to describe it. "I remember seeing something like it on a crime show I watched with the security folks when I was younger. The handle had an eerie-looking oval shape with dark patches—almost looked like a face. And below the oval were two bones—at least they appeared to be bones—crossing each other." She laid one paw over the other at angles. "Like this."

I repeated her description to Gloria, and we both sat there for a moment, processing. Our brains were busy trying to unravel the mystery of Kevin's tattoo, when Gloria shrieked, "A skull and crossbones!"

"Oh, yes, of course. A pirate symbol. And maybe it wasn't a knife but a dagger. Kevin's ship captain name was Silver Dagger."

"Interesting," Gloria managed. "I'm still sad he's gone though. He seemed like such a nice young man."

Zoe said something to Snow, and she finally said, "Snow says he may not have been at work like he was at home."

Hmmm. I wondered what he meant by that, but then again, this was coming from a cat.

Either way, we had ventured into unchartered territory and suddenly had a body, a missing boat, a fight, and lots of pirate symbology to wade through.

ZOE

Snow and I headed back to the clowder after we finished talking to Cat and Gloria. I hadn't yet introduced him to everyone, and I wondered if it would help distract him from his loss.

"Are you okay?" I checked in with him as we made our way across the courtyard. "Hungry? We could grab a bite to eat on our way?" I stopped and lifted my nose to the air, trying to detect any prey.

"I'm perfectly fine," he insisted. "Why?"

"Because your biped is gone?"

"Oh." He seemed completely unfazed. "I'll get over it."

"Apparently."

I had never been "owned" by a biped, nor did I really believe in the whole ownership thing, but I felt like, if I had a biped looking after me, providing me with food and shelter, I might grow somewhat fond of them. And if something happened to them, well, it might affect me in some kind of way.

I wasn't sure cats really got depressed or sad like bipeds did, but we did have some feelings.

We definitely experienced joy. And anger. And boredom. And jealousy.

"So, you are friends with those bipeds?" he asked, changing the subject.

"Well, 'friends' is a strong word. We are more like associates."

"You can communicate with them though?" He seemed genuinely curious.

"Cat and I can communicate. I don't know why or how. That's too much for my feline brain to wrap itself around, but I hear her, and she apparently hears me, and we understand each other."

"Interesting. I think you like them more than you're letting on," he observed.

I scoffed. "Who cares? The point is, if the wrong bipeds find out about Kevin's body being discovered in the park, especially since he was there at the same time as guests, this place is gonna get shut down, and then where will that leave us?"

Once again, he didn't seem concerned. "Well, I don't plan to stay."

I stared at him. "What do you mean? There's a fence. You can't just leave."

"Oh, I'll figure something out. I'm very resourceful."

We had arrived at the bushes my clowder called home. Hank was there to greet us.

"Hank, this is Snow. Snow, this is Hank. Where is everyone?" I glanced around, trying to spot ears, tails or paws.

Hank lazily rolled onto his belly and wiggled his back against the ground, apparently scratching an itch of some sort. "Don't know. Don't care. I've been asleep all night."

"Did you eat?" I asked him.

"Yeah, had a bite earlier. Little mouse family came walking right into my trap." He smiled deviously.

"A whole family? Geez, Hank." I turned to Snow. "He likes to set out bait—usually some food a park guest has dropped, and then he ambushes the mice who try to take it. Quite clever and takes almost zero effort on his part."

Snow gave Hank a once-over. "I like your style."

"So, everyone else is gone?" I asked again.

"Moony, Priss and Ziti are around. Those two mollies are gaga over your brother." He chuckled.

I tapped my paw impatiently on the ground. "Yeah. I'm aware."

I had wanted to do something about it, but now that Snow was here, he was serving quite nicely in the role of my second—the role that should belong to Moony. Well, if Moony was going to screw around with those two silly females, then he could just go ahead and give up his rank in the clowder. What did I care?

Snow said he would just leave, but he didn't know how good we had it here. It was a feline paradise—plenty of food if you were a good hunter, and very little biped interference.

The only real issue we had was Scar and his bunch of morons.

Snow plopped down under the bush and stretched out for a moment. Then his head popped up. "You know what? I could actually go for a morsel or two." He turned toward me with a smirk. "Feel like a hunt?"

I licked my lips with anticipation. "Thought you'd never ask."

Eleven

CATHERINE

Two days later, we'd stalled out on our investigation, though I had two days off after my shift, and I would be trying to find the boat that capsized and look for clues in the area where it happened. But when I got to work that night, Mr. Forest called me to the conference room in the Guest Services building. He said Gloria could come as well.

When we entered the building, Jayden and Nora were holding the elevator for us, so we all rode up together. "Well, what is your dad going to say?" I asked him.

Jayden smiled. "The detectives are going to be there to discuss what they've found so far. And Dad wants us to share our information with them."

"Ah, okay." I exchanged a glance with Gloria, and I could tell by her expression she knew exactly what I was thinking. Why should we do all the work and turn our hard-earned information over to them?

And the way her expression shifted right after, I knew she was thinking that we should do it to protect the park from closure and, you know, for the greater good.

Oh, yeah.

I didn't know why sleuthing made me so territorial, but it was clearly fulfilling some deep-seated need for excitement that had been missing from my life for some time. I wasn't sharing what Zoe and Snow told me though. Obviously they wouldn't believe me anyway.

They'd probably haul me off to the nearest psychiatric facility.

"Hi, Mr. Forest, Mrs. Forest, Detective Towers," I greeted everyone as we entered the conference room. They all stood to greet us and shake our hands.

"Can I get y'all anything?" Mrs. Forest asked as we all settled around the table. She had one of those old-money Charleston accents that sounded so gracious and refined, like sipping a mint julep on an antebellum porch.

"Can you get some water from the fridge in the lounge?" Mr. Forest asked.

"Sure, honey. Just a moment." She cast her beaming beauty-pageant smile around the table and then went off to procure the refreshments. I had a feeling she'd bring back more than just water.

"I'm going to turn this over to Detective Towers." Mr. Forest gestured to the detective, who looked overheated in her navy pantsuit. I wondered where her partner was, Mr. Powers, but I wasn't a big fan so I wasn't missing him or anything. I was sure Shelly Towers could handle this case on her own just fine.

"Thank you, Mr. Forest." She nodded at him and glanced around the room as she delivered her report, "As you know, we recovered Kevin Morris's body from under the bridge. The preliminary report is back from the Medical Examiner, but we're still waiting on the tox screen and the full official report. What I can tell you is that Mr. Morris did drown."

There was a collective sigh of relief as we all assumed that eliminated the possibility of him being murdered.

"However," she continued, "the ME found significant abrasions and contusions consistent with blunt-force trauma, so it's possible the force of the blow or repeated blows knocked him unconscious before he entered the water, and that caused him to drown. So we are not ruling out foul play."

I thought back to the fight Snow described on the boat. Did someone on the boat hit Kevin with something? Who was it? Why were they on the boat in the first place?

"Now we're in the process of establishing a timeline from after Kevin clocked out from his shift here to when his body was found. The ME believes Kevin died within twenty-four hours after he clocked out. So, what happened within that timeframe, and how did he end up in the water? What was he hit with? The largest bruise on his body was in an odd shape, so we are trying to determine what might have caused it."

"What kind of shape?" I spoke up.

"I don't have a copy of the preliminary report with me," Detective Towers answered. "But I can share the official report when it is available. It will be coming soon."

I nodded. Surely this meant the police were already investigating the area outside the park where the tributary inside the park met the Ashley River. Why did it disappoint me to think I would likely find nothing if I went there myself? I was planning to do that tomorrow on my day off.

"It's important you let me know what evidence you've found—no matter how trivial or circumstantial it might be—in the park," Detective Towers pleaded. "I want to keep the lines of communication open. If there are employees here in the park who knew Kevin and might be considered suspects, I want to interview them."

Mr. Forest's gaze snapped to mine. "Catherine, do you have any leads for Detective Towers?"

I cleared my throat. I had to decide what to share and decide fast. Mr. Forest already knew what we'd found at The Wizard's Spell, so I had to admit that much.

"First we talked to Bree Townsend, who works in the kitchen at Dragon's Lair Pizza. She is Kevin's ex-girlfriend. She told us he plays a game at a shop in Charleston his uncle owns called The Wizard's Spell. He just broke up with her recently. We went to the store after finding Bree's stolen figurine from the game Kevin plays, which is called Prisons & Pirates. He was the leader of the game, the one who facilitates the action. The position is called a ship captain. Apparently, outside of work and in the game, Kevin went by the name of The Silver Dagger."

The detective's eyes widened as she furiously scribbled notes. "Wow, okay. So what did you find out at the store?"

Jayden took over. "Nora and I went, posing as nerds."

There was a slight chuckle.

"We joined the new P 'n P game—apparently they started a new one after Kevin's disappearance, and this one was led by Stevie Morris, Kevin's cousin. He is the new ship captain and apparently goes by Drago."

"Isn't that from *Rocky IV*?" Detective Towers asked.

"Yeah, well…that's what he wanted us to call him," Jayden explained.

"I spoke to Steve Morris, Kevin's uncle, who didn't have much to say, just that his brother and sister-in-law were worried about their son," I added.

"I spoke with his parents yesterday," the detective revealed. "They are absolutely devastated. They had no idea what he had gotten himself into. They said it seemed like a cult, that he'd become obsessed with weapons and had gotten a huge tattoo on his back. I didn't realize it was a game at his uncle's store. They didn't tell me that."

"That seems odd to me," I remarked, thinking of the tattoo Zoe had described. "Wouldn't they know he was playing at his uncle's shop?"

The detective shrugged. "It's almost like he kept his Silver Dagger persona completely separate from his real life. No one here at the park knew about it except Bree, right?"

"I think Nathan, who works with Bree, knew," I shared. "When we went to talk to Bree the first time, he was protective of her and said some disparaging things about Kevin."

"So is he a suspect too?" Mr. Forest shook his head. "I can't believe this is the caliber of employees I've got working for me."

I felt terrible for him. He seemed to be a good person and to care about his employees, not just about the bottom line. Not to mention the threat these murders were posing to his livelihood. All of our livelihoods, really. But I could get a janitorial job anywhere. What does someone who has only run a theme park for his entire adult life do if it all falls apart?

His wife finally returned carrying a huge tray of snacks and what looked like a cooler. "Here, everyone, I put together a little something for you." She set the tray in the middle of the table. There were cookies, brownies, and little bags of chips. "I'll be right back with the coffee."

We all suspended our conversation as she carried in an enormous coffee urn and plugged it in. She pulled out some mugs from a cabinet below the counter, and took a carton of creamer from the cooler, which was also full of water bottles and cans of soda.

I had a feeling she was going to turn up with a ton of goodies for us.

"Back to Nathan—he's only a kid. Doesn't mean he's not capable of murder," I noted, "but it doesn't seem likely.

"Anyone else in the park involved in the game?" the detective asked. "Since his body was found here, and he likely died near the park, I have to wonder if someone who works here was involved."

"It's possible the blunt-force trauma came from an object he hit in the water?" Gloria interjected. "Something not wielded by a person?"

"It's possible," Detective Towers stated, "but not likely. If we can figure out what the imprint on his forehead is, that would help a lot."

"I really need to see a picture of it." Maybe that was something I could look for on my days off. It could have been the murder weapon. "If someone hit him, and he ended up in the water and drowned, is it still murder?"

Detective Towers sighed. "It depends on the circumstances and the motive. There are certainly a lot of unanswered questions at this point."

"Agreed. Well, we'll be on the lookout for clues," I promised, and Gloria nodded in agreement. Jayden and Nora did too.

My little band of sleuths had grown. Now we'd have to

see if four heads were better than two. Or would it be "five heads are better than three..."? After all, I couldn't forget Zoe in all this.

She might have broken the case wide open when she found that figurine. What else was she capable of finding?

ZOE

It was a quiet night in the park. All of the bipeds working seemed to be inside. I hardly saw anyone walking around. It might have been because it had been pouring rain off and on all evening.

My clowder and I had retreated to the interior of the castle to stay dry. It was the first time we'd all been together since Snow arrived. We were all watching Priss and Ziti's hissing, shrieky catfight to impress Moony when Cat and Gloria came rushing into the castle.

"Oh, you are in here!" Cat exclaimed when she saw us.

I walked to the center of the atrium, where there was a beautiful round inlay of wood with a fancy light hanging over it. "Everyone, quiet! I need to be able to hear Cat."

Everyone immediately went silent, and pride surged through me. My clowder had been a little off the rails in the past week or two, but I still had some semblance of control. Everyone sat quietly, Priss and Ziti flanking Moony as if they were his personal bodyguards.

"Thank you." Cat stepped forward. "We need your help."

"What else is new?" I shot back.

"Well, yes, but you know what's at stake."

"What have you found out about the biped?" I questioned.

"He was hit in the head with something before he fell off the boat. Your friend said there was a fight but didn't know any details. Well, we need details. My colleague Jayden tried to find the spot where the boat might have launched and look for clues around the area, but it's all blocked off by police tape. And there were officers on the scene, so he couldn't sneak by them."

"Well, can't the police do what they're supposed to do?" Seemed like some of these bipeds were just as incompetent as certain felines.

"They could," I said, "but they don't have all the info we have. I didn't tell them about the boat. They're just trying to figure out how Kevin got into the water and where the injury happened. They don't know to look for evidence from a boat."

I sighed. "So what do you want me to do about it?"

"Well…I was hoping you could figure out a way to get up river—you know, under or over the fence—and see if you can find anything from the boat or maybe locate the object that was used to hit him."

I looked into her eyes. Because of the glare from her glasses, I'd never realized her eyes almost looked like a cat's. But I could see them clearly now—no glare. "What kind of object?"

She glanced at Gloria and then back to me. "We're not entirely sure, but something that could have left an odd-shaped mark on his forehead."

"So let me get this straight," I said. "You want me to figure out a way to get out of the park and look for something, but you don't even know what it is?"

When I put it like that, it sounded pretty ridiculous, didn't it? Also, was she forgetting we were cats? Though we had several advantages over bipeds, we were small and didn't win the evolutionary lottery in the opposable thumb department. We weren't experts on biped paraphernalia. Most of what I knew came from TV shows—which bipeds fully admit aren't particularly realistic. This sounded like a job for bipeds, not felines.

"If you can't figure out how to do it, then fine. I just thought maybe we could speed the investigation up, try to keep it from leaking to the public. You know, like last time. But if it's asking too much, then we'll figure out another way," she said. "If you're not capable of getting over there, maybe I'll ask Jayden and Nora to try going back to the scene at nighttime."

Whoa, hold up. Is she issuing me a challenge? Insinuating I'm not capable of completing this task?

Just because a biped might be able to do it easier and faster didn't mean I wasn't perfectly capable of doing it too.

"I'll give you a full report as soon as we get back." I turned to Moony and Snow. "Get ready. We're leaving as soon as Cat and Gloria do."

Priss and Ziti approached me, begging to go along with us.

"Just me, Moony and Snow," I insisted, much to their dismay. I was pretty sure they'd follow Moony off a cliff if he led them there. "Cat, can you meet me back here later tonight?"

She looked at Gloria, who nodded. "You'll be okay in the rain?"

"Well, we're not made of sugar," I retorted. "We won't melt. C'mon, boys."

Twelve

The rain let up by the time we got over to the Water Fairy Adventure ride. Moony and Snow were arguing the entire way about the best plan for getting outside the park. Since Snow was the only one who had actually been outside the park under his own power—Moony had merely been captured and returned; he literally had no say in any of it—I tended to give him a little more credence.

While Snow went up ahead to see where the fence was at the edge of park property as well as its height, I took a moment to talk to my brother in private.

"What is your deal, Moony? You've been absolutely insufferable since those two mollies started competing for your affection," I confronted him.

He puffed out his chest. "Insufferable…or awesome?"

"Definitely insufferable." I paced in a small circle while I collected my thoughts. "Look, I understand why you are feeling a certain amount of pride that you have two lovely ladies vying for your attention, but you have to get your head out of your rear end and get back to helping me run this clowder. We must ensure that Scar and his minions don't take over the whole park. You were supposed to help me with the River Cats, and you never did."

He looked a little solemn, maybe even remorseful sitting there with his tail curled around his long gray and white fur. Cats rarely took responsibility for their mistakes, but it almost looked as though I might be getting through to him.

Yet he was silent on the matter.

I kept pacing. "Can you just choose one of them so we can all get on with our lives?" I sat right in front of him, close enough for our whiskers to touch. "I order you to choose."

"You can't do that." He bared his teeth and stuck his tongue out, giving me the softest hiss. "You don't have that kind of authority."

"Do you want to lose your position in our clowder? Because you will. I will put Snow in your place so fast, you won't even know what hit you."

He didn't back down. "That's not fair, Zoe, and you know it. You're just jealous that I have admirers."

I looked off in the distance to see if Snow was on his way back yet. It always seemed like he was flirting with me. Maybe he counted as an admirer?

"Besides, you know we can't mate anyway. All the felines here get fixed, and you know it. No kittens for the Felines of Fairytale Forest," he reminded me.

"We still form bonds," I shot back. "If you want to be attached to a female, fine. Then choose one. And if you don't, you're just playing games with them, and that's not fair to either of them."

He considered that for a moment as Snow appeared above the berm. He looked like he'd seen a monster, flying toward us, his paws pounding into the ground.

"What's wrong?" I asked as he arrived beside us, panting, his fur standing on end.

"There are cats down there," he gasped for air, "blocking the exit." He was clearly not used to running. I was sure he was served store-bought cat food in a fancy dish.

"What do you mean?" My eyes bounced between his.

"There are five or six big toms," he explained. "They wouldn't let me pass."

"Not the River Cats?" Was there another clowder who lived on the river that I didn't know about?

"No." He shook his head. "None of the quiet, meek cats you introduced me to a few days ago. These toms were mean. Really foul, actually."

Moony and I looked at each other, our nostrils flaring. "Scar," we both said in unison.

But why?

I started marching down toward the park boundary while Snow and Moony stayed frozen on the riverbank. Finally, I heard them racing up behind me, breathing hard.

"What do you think you're doing, Sis?" Moony asked as he fell in stride beside me.

"I'm sick and tired of those goons interfering in everyone else's business. They are not going to prevent me from keeping my promise to Cat, nor are they going to stop me from keeping the park safe from closure. We're going to figure something out, some way to get around them. I'm not going to let them intimidate me."

"But we're outnumbered," Snow said. "There were like six of them, and they were huge. They looked ready to rumble. I don't particularly want to risk getting hurt."

He sounded like a spoiled, entitled jerk. Why didn't I see this before? He clearly wasn't as awesome as I thought.

"I thought you liked adventure," I threw over my shoulder at him. He was having a hard time keeping up. *I'm sure he's used to sitting around all day and being fed treats. He's never had to work for his meals like we do*, I reasoned.

"Sure, I like adventure very much," he argued. "When I'm not going to risk my neck."

I refused to stop. "Then go on, get out of here. I don't need help from someone with that attitude."

He raced in front of me and put his paw out to stop me. "Wait, Zoe."

"What?" I was panting, my chest heaving as I struggled to breathe in the thick, wet air.

"I care about you," he said. "I don't want you to get hurt either. I don't know who those other cats are, but they seemed very unreasonable. They hissed at me and showed their claws. Once they started to stalk me, I got the heck out of there. Sorry, but I don't want them to attack you or your brother. You two don't deserve that."

"We have to solve the mystery," I reminded him. "Our way of life is at stake. I understand why you don't feel a personal sense of investment, but we do. And their hiss is worse than their bite. Trust me, they were just trying to intimidate you."

"Could we get more numbers?" Moony asked. "I could run back to the clowder and see if Ice, Ziti and Amber are around."

They were my other three best fighters and hunters.

Cool would probably want to come too, but hopefully Hank, Priss, and Daisy could convince him to stay. I didn't know where Sass was or if she'd be any help at all. I still wasn't completely sure I could trust her, especially where Scar's mafia was concerned.

I thought about Moony's suggestion for a short time. But my mind was made up quickly. "No. I'm tired of this mousecrap. C'mon, let's roll. You're either with me or against me!"

I marched forward, not caring if these two were following me or not. I was angry enough to override any good sense I may have otherwise had. I already went and confronted Vinny on his and Scar's turf earlier this week, and now it was time to prove they couldn't bully me off their turf either.

We stealthily approached the edge of a grassy area that dropped off to the river below. It was only a drop of about three or four feet—not nearly as far as the jump I made with Snow off the boat on the Water Fairy Adventure ride. I needed to get my bearings before I allowed the six cats patrolling the sandy area beside the river to see us.

The river flowing into the park was wide here, and it looked shallow. It was indeed a branch of the bigger river beyond. There was only a tiny space for us to crouch and possibly jump down onto the sandy area before a tall fence rose into the sky. The metal fence was too tall for us to scale, so this small space was our only hope of accessing the area where Scar's thugs were.

I looked across the smaller branch of the river and saw where the fence began again. There was nothing over the river. I supposed, if there wasn't a track, you could maneuver one of those fairy boats right out to the bigger river outside the park. But they were on a track, and I didn't think they would be easy to move off it. They might not even float for all I knew.

Then I looked across to the land on the other side of the bigger river. There was yellow ribbon wrapped around the trees blocking off a wide area, and I couldn't see where the ribbon ended. There was black lettering—biped writing—on the yellow, but obviously I couldn't read it. It was too dark to see anything else over there from this far away, but the yellow ribbon stood out in the moonlight.

I needed to figure out a way to get over there. But the river was wide, and there was nothing to help cross it, at least nothing I could see from here. I'd have to get down there closer to make out anything else.

"I have a plan," I whispered to my comrades.

They both looked at me, waiting for instructions.

Okay, it wasn't so much of a plan as it was a starting point. But they didn't need to know that.

"We're all going to jump down there, and you're going to distract them while I cross the river," I explained.

"Are you out of your mind?" my brother hissed. "That's the worst plan I've ever heard! You do know there are six of them and two of us, right?"

"I agree that plan sounds misguided," Snow contributed.

"Fine," I hissed back. "Then I'm going to just jump down there and do it myself. You two can sit here and look pretty."

I started to get in position to leap down when my brother put his paw on my tail. "Stop it," I gritted out between clenched teeth. "I'm doing this, and I don't really care what you think."

"You're gonna get hurt, Zoe. Didn't you see the cats down there? It's Vinny, Gill, Frank, Alfie, Tony and Claw. They're Scar's best fighters!"

"Don't care," I repeated.

After taking a deep breath to work up the appropriate level of audacity, I used my back paws to spring off the grassy area, sailing through the air and landing in thick reeds that would conceal me while I formulated the next stage of my plan.

"Who goes there?" Vinny shouted.

The only answer was crickets chirping and bullfrogs croaking in the damp, drizzly night.

"We're guarding this river bank," Vinny continued. "No one can come or go except through us."

Not so much as a soft mew rolled out of my mouth as I glanced above me at the grassy spot where we'd been hiding next to the fence. My brother and Snow were now gone.

What the toe beans are they doing? Just abandoning me? Figures.

Deep breaths, I coached myself. *Don't panic.*

I needed to figure out how to get across the river. Scanning the water, I found it was rushing much faster after all the summer rains we'd received in the past few weeks. It was dark and churning, and it was hard to make out any details.

Then the clouds parted, and the full brightness of the moon shone down on the river, lighting it up. There were a few rocks and what looked like a log that I might be able to use to make my way across.

Okay, first I just had to make it past these goons. I was perfectly capable of that, right?

I got down low like I was stalking prey. My butt began to wiggle as I summoned all my strength and speed—I'd need both to make it across. I planned to bolt across the small beach like lightning. They wouldn't even know what hit them.

Then I thought I heard something behind me, and the blood inside me froze.

"And what do we have here?" came a sneer from the other side of the reeds.

Mouse turds!

"Oh, hi, Vinny…"

The tuxedo cat stepped back, allowing me to step forward into the light. Apparently the water wasn't the only thing the moon illuminated when it showed up. It gave away my position too.

"And where do you think you're going?" Vinny asked as his six goons surrounded us.

"Pretty molly like you out here alone?" Gill dug one of his front paws into the sand as his eyes roamed over me. "Not very smart, Z."

"I need to get to the other side of the river," I explained.

"Why?" Vinny demanded. Six pairs of glowing eyes drilled into me.

"I'm looking for something," I explained. "Did you meet my friend Snow? That white cat who showed up a few days ago? His boat wrecked, and he lost his collar. I'm trying to find it for him. He floated into the park from right here."

It wasn't a lie. Well, the collar part was a lie, but the rest was true. Not bad for making it up on the fly, right?

"Well, we can't let you pass," Vinny ruled, and his goons tightened their circle around me.

This was really starting to tick me off!

"This is not your territory, Vinny. This isn't even the park. We are off park property right now!" I seethed.

"It's all Scar's territory, Z. That's where your pretty little head seems to be confused. Scar has big dreams, cupcake. And a little furball like you isn't going to stand in the way of them."

Cupcake? That was it. It'd had it.

"Hi-ya!!!" I shouted and karate-chopped my way through the blockade with my claws extended and teeth bared. I'd learned about karate from some movie I watched with the Security bipeds, and I never thought it would be applicable to my real life, but here we were.

They started to chase after me when I heard, "Hi-ya!" from the top of the bank.

I bounded onto the nearest rock in the river, my legs shaking and my paws struggling to hold on to the wet stone. When I turned around to see the scene unfolding from the bank, Snow, Moony and six River Cats were leaping onto the beach and surprising the whiskers off Vinny and his not-so-merry band of thugs.

"Yes! Way to go, Moony! You show them who's boss!" I yelled across the churning river.

I was so invigorated by their sudden appearance that I was caught-off guard by a rush of water that knocked me clean off the rock. I hit the water with a scream, the chill taking my breath away.

I fought my way up through the current to take a breath, but I was not made for this. I was not a fish or a frog or a turtle. I was a long-haired domestic feline, for meowing out loud!

And even worse—I didn't think anyone on the beach even noticed I'd fallen in.

I didn't know if I would be able to claw my way out of this predicament.

I knew from my whiskers to the tip of my tail that this could very well be the end...

Thirteen

CATHERINE

Those cats never made it back to meet with us. I hoped they didn't get trapped outside the park. Gloria and I walked extra slow through the courtyard to make sure we didn't see them hiding out in their home bushes.

"I'm sure they're fine," Gloria assured me. "They probably either couldn't get over there, or they didn't find anything."

"It's just not like Zoe. She was so dependable when we were working on the other case. Now I'm going to be off for two days, and I'm going to worry about her the entire time."

"Spoken like a true mom," Gloria said with a laugh. "Why don't we drive over to where we think the park river meets the Ashley River? We can scope it out for ourselves and look for her. The police are probably gone by now."

It never ceased to amaze me how much energy Gloria had. She was about ten years older than me, and I swore she never got tuckered out. I wished I could borrow just a small percentage of it. "You don't need to get home for anything else?"

"Dog has four feet, but can only walk one road, Cat," she quoted a Gullah proverb.

"And that means?" I raised an eyebrow at my friend.

"Gotta focus on one thing at a time," she said, "and right now it's this case. Isn't that what you're gonna do today?" She raised an eyebrow right back at me.

"Well," I looked ahead toward the park exit, "I was gonna take a nap, maybe try to get four hours of sleep. Then I was gonna try to track down Kevin Morris's parents."

"Detective Towers already spoke to them, right?" Gloria asked.

"Yes, but I think we can ask them better questions," I said. "And we'll go over there as coworkers to express our condolences, ask them when his services are. I think we'll get a fair bit more insight than the police did."

"That makes sense. Do you want company?" She fluttered her eyelashes at me.

"Yeah, sure. I was going to ask Jayden and Nora if they had any ideas about how to talk to Stevie Morris. Because he is next on my list."

Gloria's face lit up. She obviously liked working with the two teens. "Are they off today and tomorrow as well?"

I grinned. "They are. I am hoping to solve this case before we come back to work. And before anything is leaked to the media."

"From your lips to God's ears!" She pointed to the sky as we made our way down Storybook Street.

"Do you think this is the best place to park?" I pulled up to the edge of the gravel lot and put my Nissan Rogue in park.

"Where are we?" Gloria looked out the windshield, then her window and then back at me. "I feel like we're in the middle of nowhere."

I reached for my phone and zoomed out on my maps app. There were tiny tributaries off the Ashley River and swampland all over the place, which made it difficult to get anywhere. "From what I can tell, this little park is across the river from the Fairytale Forest boundary."

"Well, let's see what we can find then." Gloria opened her door and got out. I grabbed my phone, purse and keys and followed.

"Oh, let me grab a grocery bag in case we need to carry any evidence out. And I've got a pair of gloves in my purse." I opened the back end of my Rogue with the key fob.

"You must have been a Girl Scout," Gloria teased me as we walked to the edge of the small parking lot. There was a picnic table in a clearing to our right, and to our left were pine trees and thick brush, but there was a narrow hiking trail weaving between trees. It smelled like fresh pine needles. I sucked in a deep breath of it, filling my lungs with piney goodness.

"I was a Girl Scout. Don't be a hater," I retorted.

Gloria sniffed the air. "I'm not a hater, but I can one-up you. I feel the spirit of my ancestors here by the river. I can just imagine the ladies coming here to collect sweet grass to weave baskets, can't you?"

I smiled. "They probably still do."

"Darn right they do." She flashed me a proud grin.

We followed the path through the woods, assuming it would come out at the river. We were not wrong, but the entire area was cordoned off with yellow crime tape. "Guess Jayden was right. But there's no one here, so I say we just do our thing. We're in cahoots with the detective, after all."

"True," Gloria agreed, and I lifted the caution tape while she limboed underneath it. Then I did the same as she held it.

"Would you look at that?" I pointed across the river to an offshoot flanked by two tall metal fences. "That has to be the park, right?"

Gloria squinted. "I do believe you are correct."

When my eyes roved over the sandy bank, they landed on a disturbing sight.

It was a lump of gray fur.

"Gloria!" I shrieked as I rushed over to the lump. My friend was right on my heels.

I dropped to the ground on my knees like my body wasn't riddled with arthritis. "Zoe?" I stroked down the gray fur, holding my breath as I imagined the very worst.

Moments later, a furry gray head lifted off the sand.

"Zoe!" I scooped her up into my arms.

As any feral cat would do, she scratched the crap out of my arm. "Ouch!"

I dropped her to the ground, and she shook herself off, her eyes slowly blinking as she got her bearings. "Cat?" she mewed groggily.

"Oh my gosh, I thought you were dead!" I exclaimed, still on my knees. I was never getting up from this spot, was I?

Gloria stood over me. "Is she okay? What happened to her?"

"Just a sec…" I lifted a finger to request a moment. Then I realized Zoe was lying beside what looked like a water-logged athletic shoe.

I picked it up. Why did it look familiar to me? It was a brand I'd never heard of and the white leather was quite stained with dirt.

"I found that." Zoe walked a few feet, turned in a circle and then made her way back to me, her tail shaking in the morning breeze.

"How did you get over here?" I stuffed the shoe inside the shopping bag I'd brought with me.

"I swam…I think." She still looked pretty disoriented. *Poor thing.*

"What can I do for you?" I was worried about her. And I felt guilty all over again. I was the one who asked her to come over here and check things out.

"Don't worry about me. I'll be fine. Just don't know how I'll get back to my clowder." She went to the edge of the river and peered across at the fence where the park lay beyond.

"I'll take care of that," I promised. "But I'm off work the next two nights."

"Well, I can't wait that long." She sat up on her haunches, looking serious.

Gloria was walking along the edge of the river, bent over as she scanned the reeds and dirt for clues. "Hey…I think there's something over here, but I'm not sure I can reach it."

We both walked over to her. She pointed in the water where something shiny lay in the rocks of the riverbed.

"I'll get it." It didn't look that deep here, so I took off my socks and shoes and waded out into the water. "Mmm… feels kinda nice, actually."

"Really? It was cold last night," Zoe claimed.

I reached down to feel for the shiny object, but walking around stirred up the sediment and made the water cloudy. It was only up to my knees, but deep enough that I couldn't see the bottom now.

Then my bare foot hit something sharp. "Ouch!"

I lifted my foot out of the water to see a rivulet of blood drip into the water. "Well, great, now I have a cut on my foot to match the scratch you gave me on my arm, Zoe." The scratch stung as I reached down into the water to try to grasp the object without cutting myself again.

Gloria gasped. "Is that what I think it is?"

Zoe took one look at it and said, "The tattoo on Kevin's back—it was of that."

In my hands was a small keychain—a silver dagger with a skull and crossbones on the handle. And the dagger was SHARP as all get out. How could you carry that thing around in your pocket without cutting yourself? There were keys attached: one to a Chevy truck, what looked like house keys, and some others that might have belonged to Fairytale Forest. I put the set in the bag along with the shoe, and we made our way back to the car, Zoe on our heels.

Fourteen

CATHERINE

I thought it would be hard to find Kevin's parents' house, but it wasn't at all. First, I remembered Kevin had been Employee of the Month in June. I found the email with the company newsletter, which included a little interview and biography. It started with, "Kevin is the son of Stanley and Elizabeth Morris, Johns Island." I also remembered the detective saying his parents lived out on Johns Island.

So, I googled their names and Johns Island, South Carolina, and found their address with no issue whatsoever. But before we headed out there, we stopped at a florist to buy an arrangement so we could properly convey our condolences. I stayed in the car with Zoe while Gloria picked it out since she had better taste in such things than I did.

We drove southwest to Johns Island and pulled into the Morrises' driveway. It was a stucco ranch painted a terracotta color with ivory shutters and trim. Neatly trimmed hedges surrounded the front porch, and there were hanging baskets of geraniums.

I turned to look in the back seat, where a lovely long-haired gray cat was perched all prim and proper-like. You'd never know she'd endured an ordeal the night before, washing up on a riverbank. "Okay, Zoe, I need your help."

"What now?" she practically groaned, which I didn't even realize cats could do.

"I'm going to put you inside the shopping bag and set you down in the house while we talk to the Morrises. You can scour the house for clues, but you need to be super sneaky about it. I'm particularly interested in any receipts from Walmart. I know Kevin went to Walmart the morning after his shift—"

"But he didn't live with them," Gloria reminded me. "So why would his receipt be here? Do we even know if he really went? I thought it was just a rumor."

"I don't know! I heard it from someone. Ugh! It doesn't hurt to look." I was grasping at straws. This case was more complex than the last one. We knew a few employees hated Heather, and when we followed the clues, we got an unexpected break in the case. This case, we didn't know anyone who hated Kevin except possibly his cousin and his ex-girlfriend, but neither of them really gave off "murderer" vibes.

"What's Walmart?" Zoe piped up.

"Argghhhh!" I buried my face in my palms. I needed to think for a minute. We were sitting in these people's driveway. We couldn't exactly keep sitting here forever—they were going to get freaked out. Not what we needed if we wanted to ask them about their recently deceased son.

"Zoe, just let me know if you find anything interesting,

any slips of paper or anything to do with pirates." She started to grumble, but I just scooped her up. "Into the bag you go now. Be quiet!"

Gloria stifled her laughter with her hand, and we both exited the Rogue. She retrieved the beautiful planter she chose at the florist, and we made our way up to the porch. I rang the doorbell, my purse and the shopping bag slung over my shoulder.

So much for getting any sleep this morning, right? Maybe if we were super lucky, Mrs. Morris would offer us some coffee, but I didn't expect any southern hospitality from a woman who just lost her son. I was sure she was still beside herself with grief.

A woman about my age answered the door wearing what looked like workout clothes. Her gray-streaked brown hair was pulled into a ponytail high on her head, and she wore a pink sweatband. "Can I help you?" She smiled sweetly.

"Um...Mrs. Morris?" She was not what I was expecting...

"Yes?" She didn't open the door any further than her face, which was understandable since she had two strangers standing on her porch.

"Honey, who is it?" called a male voice behind her. She swung the door open to reveal a middle-aged man wearing a fitted navy-blue tank top and athletic shorts. He was in quite good shape.

It looked like we had interrupted their morning workout. *Oops!*

"Hi, I'm Catherine Lyon, and this is Gloria Bress. We worked with your son at Fairytale Forest, and we've come to pay our respects," I announced. Gloria lifted the planter up, which was artfully arranged in a white wicker basket.

"Oh…" She turned to look at the man I presumed was her husband. "Okay. Well, you can come in if you'd like."

Gloria and I both nodded and smiled, following her into the modern-looking living room with white furniture and a sleek flat-screen TV hanging on the wall. The window was filled with planters—ours would look right at home.

She took the basket from Gloria. "This is beautiful, thank you. I'll put it over here with the others. Would you guys like some coffee?"

She did not have a southern accent. She sounded like she was from New York, the way she said "coffee."

"That would be delightful," Gloria answered for me because I was too busy thanking my lucky stars that coffee was about to happen. *I may survive after all.*

The man I presumed to be Mr. Morris ushered us toward the sofa, and we both sat down. "I'm Stanley Morris. It's nice to meet some of my son's coworkers. I'm going to go help Liz with the coffee, and we'll be right back. Make yourselves at home."

We both expressed our gratitude, and I carefully set my bag down on the floor beside the sofa, as far back as I could reach, hoping Zoe would be able to slip out discreetly. I didn't hear a sound, and when I checked a few seconds later, she was already gone. I just hoped she didn't have any trouble getting back into the bag before we had to leave.

It didn't take long for the Morrises to return with two mugs of coffee and a tray filled with creamer and various sweeteners. We both fixed our coffees the way we liked them and settled back on the sofa while our hosts took the loveseat.

"I'm Liz," the woman introduced herself. "Sorry if I didn't say before. I've been a little scatterbrained with everything going on."

"Perfectly understandable," I said before taking a sip of the coffee. Holy cow, it was good. So freaking good. "We're so sorry for your loss. Your son was a bright spot of our shift every time we saw him."

"He was always friendly and made an effort to speak to us," Gloria added. "We're just so sad to hear he's no longer with us."

Liz nodded sadly. "My stepson was a fine young man. Quiet, though. So quiet."

Hmm. She's his stepmother, not his mother. Noted.

Stan Morris sat stoically beside his wife holding one of those fancy water bottles that keeps your water cold for weeks on end. I needed to figure out how to ask him about his brother's game store without it being weird.

I was good at weird.

Not so good at not weird.

"We recently met Bree Townsend at the park," I began. "She said she used to date Kevin—"

"Bree is such a nice girl. She lives just down the street from us, actually. She and Kevin went to high school together, and he always had the biggest crush on her. He was so shy, he only got the confidence to ask her out earlier this summer..." Liz looked wistfully out the window while her husband remained silent.

"I'm sure they made a nice couple." I needed to steer the conversation a little bit more... "She said she played a game with Kevin at The Wizard's Spell in Charleston..."

"Yes, that's my brother-in-law's store," Liz answered. No contribution from Mr. Morris.

"Did you know much about the game they played? Prisons & Pirates?" I pressed a little harder.

"We knew he played some pirate game, and we thought it was just at the store on Thursday nights... We didn't realize it was more than that." She looked at her husband as if asking for corroboration, but he continued to stare straight ahead.

Gloria's eyes widened, and she put one hand on my thigh momentarily. I had an opening, and I was going to run with it.

I tilted my head and met her gaze. "More than that? What do you mean?"

"Well, from what the detective told us when the police were here, it sounded like it had taken over his life. He was kind of obsessed with it," Liz explained. "We knew he got a giant pirate dagger tattoo on his back. But apparently he was also recruiting people to get into the game and, like, play pirate with him. We found out he'd been studying some fighting style that pirates used..."

"Did you know any of this before his disappearance?" I questioned.

"No," Liz shook her head, "we didn't know any of it until we started asking around when he was missing. We talked to my brother-in-law and his son, who is about Kevin's age. We talked to a couple of his friends. We didn't realize he played such a leadership role in the club of sorts. It wasn't like him. He was so quiet and shy in school and at home. Like the kind of kid who never spoke up in class and who always wanted to sort of hide in the shadows," she continued. "He was a shy, sweet, quiet kid who loved his cat and— oh, his cat is missing too, by the way... Beautiful creature.

Pure white with a striped tail. His name is Snowman. Kevin took him everywhere with him."

When I looked over at Stanley, his eyes were squeezed shut. Hearing his wife talk about Kevin was obviously very painful for him.

"At least we sort of understand now why he wanted to buy a boat." She rolled her eyes. "He didn't even know how to swim."

Gloria elbowed me, and I nearly choked at her words. *A boat?*

"Well, did he buy a boat?" I asked.

"Not that I know of. I feel like so much of his life was hidden from us, to tell you the truth. Like we didn't even know who he really was." She turned to her husband. "Don't you think, Stan?"

He nodded. "It was like he was leading a double life we knew nothing about," he finally spoke.

That had to be so painful for them. I felt just terrible about it.

I heard the tiniest rustling sound bedside me and knew it was Zoe going back into her bag.

"We still can't believe he drowned," Liz said. "I just wish I knew what he was doing in the water. The detective said he was hit by something that left an unusual mark on his face, that it might have left him unconscious and led to him drowning. I wish we knew what hit him—or if *someone* hit him."

Gloria and I exchanged looks again.

"Do you know of anyone who might have wanted to hurt him?" I followed up on her comment.

Liz and Stan exchanged looks this time. "No," Stan said flatly. "My son was quiet and reserved—he didn't have a lot of friends, but he didn't give people a reason to dislike him either."

"But he seemed to be a lot different when he played this pirate game," I reminded them. "Do you think anyone involved in the game might have had a reason to dislike him or want to hurt him?"

"Over a game?" Stan scoffed. "That's ridiculous. It's just a game."

"Right." I smiled and nodded.

"We saw Kevin right before he disappeared," Liz said. "He stopped by after work that morning. Said he needed to get something from his bedroom. He moved out last year, but he keeps a bedroom here." She shook her head. "I mean 'kept.' I don't know if we will be able to clean it out…"

"That sounds really tough. I'm sorry to hear that," I tried to sound as empathetic as possible. "Any idea where he was going after he stopped by here?"

Stan's lips thinned as if he disapproved of the question. Liz smiled, but her eyes were watery. "No, but he usually goes home to bed after his shift."

There was an awkward silence after that.

Gloria gave me a look that said we had overstayed our welcome. I stood up and extended my hand toward Mrs. Morris first. "Thank you for the coffee. Again, we're so sorry about your son. If there's anything we can do, please don't hesitate to let us know."

"His services are on Friday," Mr. Morris said when he shook my hand. "Thanks for stopping by."

WE MADE IT OUT TO THE ROGUE, AND I PEEKED INTO THE BAG to make sure Zoe was okay. She was holding something under her paw, but before I got a chance to see what it was, I heard, "Hey, you're those ladies from Fairytale Forest. You know the Morrises?"

I whipped around at the sound of the familiar voice and saw Bree Townsend standing there with a pug attached to a pink leash in her hand. Her vibrant-colored hair was blowing in the breeze, and she was wearing cut-off denim shorts and a t-shirt that said GAMER GIRL in thick letters.

"What a cute dog!" I held the shopping bag close to me, praying the dog and Zoe weren't going to smell each other and have a tussle.

"This is Zelda," she said. "Zelda, sit."

The pug obeyed. I took a step back to try to prevent any exchange of scent.

"We stopped by to give our condolences to the Morrises," Gloria explained when she realized I probably had my hands full. The bag started to move a bit, so I clutched it tighter and shot my bestie a grateful look.

"Gotcha," Bree said. "Yeah, Kevin's funeral is on Friday. I haven't decided if I'm going yet. If I see Cassidy there, I'll probably want to throat-punch her."

Well, that was...violent-sounding. But I still didn't think she'd bludgeon her ex-boyfriend over dumping her for Cassidy.

"Nathan said he'd go with me. He played in Kevin's club, you know. As did a few other guys at the park."

"They did? You mean the Prisons & Pirates game at the game shop?" I clarified.

"It went beyond that. They did some weird stuff. Like

initiation rites. And secret fighting rituals, I don't know. Only guys. Girls weren't allowed." She rolled her eyes.

"What kind of fighting rituals?" I thought about what Zoe and Snow said about the fight on the boat.

Bree shrugged. "I don't know the details. You'd have to ask Nathan or Stevie, Kevin's cousin. His dad owns The Wizard's Spell. Then there's Zach W. and Zach P. They both work day shift in park security."

"Oh, I didn't realize there were more people at the park who knew about Kevin's alter ego," I remarked.

"Yeah, well, not sure any of them want to admit to it now that Kevin's body was found in the park." Bree sighed, and Zelda started to tug on her leash.

"If we wanted to talk to Nathan…any idea how we could go about doing that?" I questioned.

"Um…I can give you his number, but it might be kinda weird." She looked wary.

"We're just trying to figure out why Kevin disappeared and then died," I explained. "You know, we're just two old ladies who like to listen to true crime podcasts. It's morbid, but this is fun for us."

"Wait, you think a crime was committed?" She blinked. "I thought he drowned. That's what we were told at work."

"Well, you just said you didn't think his coworkers at the park would want to talk to police," I shot back.

"That's not exactly what I said…" She looked down at her dog and then back up at me. Zelda was tugging on her leash, moving a little closer to me and the bag I had slung around my shoulder containing Zoe.

"Do you know something you're not telling me?" She was perceptive, wasn't she?

"No, not at all. We're probably just being silly," I assured her. "We're not detectives, obviously."

We were so totally detectives.

"Obviously," she agreed. "Fine, I'll give you Nathan's number, but I don't know if he'll talk to you." She pulled her phone out of her back pocket and scrolled through her contacts. Meanwhile, Gloria took out a slip of paper and a pen, poised to take the number down.

Bree rattled it off, and then Zelda began to growl at the shopping bag.

Oh no. We needed to get a move on!

"Great seeing you, Bree," I said as Gloria came around beside me and carefully took the shopping bag off my shoulder. She started heading toward the car as I pointed the key fob at it to unlock the doors.

Zelda followed, sniffing a mile a minute. Bree tried to jerk her back over to where she was standing, but the dog strained hard toward the car. "What's in that bag, anyway?"

"Oh, just some dirty shoes," I lied. "There's probably something smelly on them. Sorry about that. See ya later, Bree!"

She shrugged and continued to walk down the sidewalk with Zelda, crossing right in front of Kevin's house. As soon as she was out of sight, I peeked into the shopping bag. "You okay in there, Zoe?"

"Do you have any idea how difficult it was for me to restrain myself from hissing at that stupid mutt?" she asked self-righteously.

"Did you find anything in the house?" I refused to engage with her on the topic of Zelda the Pug.

"I found this. Not sure if it's what you're looking for, but it was on the floor in a bedroom down the hallway. I assume it was Kevin's. It smelled like him." She pawed at a long, narrow slip of paper in the bottom of the bag.

I lifted it out and noticed "Walmart" printed at the top. Could this really be his receipt from the morning he disappeared?

"Well, don't hold me in suspense!" Gloria begged. "What's on there?"

I read the items aloud, "Rope, flashlight, first-aid kit, bandages, and rubbing alcohol. What do you make of that?"

Her lips twisted into a frown. "Sounds like he was planning on someone getting hurt…"

Fifteen

ZOE

After I searched the bipeds' home and got harassed by a dog, Cat took me to her home. I wasn't used to being so active in the daytime, and what I really wanted to do was take a nap. She offered me a can of tuna and some water, which was much appreciated, and then I went to stretch out in the sunlight.

"Your house looks good with a cat in it," Gloria remarked as they sat in the living room near where I was basking in a sunbeam.

"It does, doesn't it?" She looked over at me. "She'd probably bite me if I tried to touch her."

Darn right I would. Cats are for looking, not touching.

There were some cats that liked to be touched, but every cat in the colony at Fairytale Forest knew that allowing a human to pet you was the first step in getting yourself exiled. No one knew what happened to the cats who got caught getting too friendly with humans. That was why my relationship with Cat and Gloria needed to be kept on the downlow. The waaaaay downlow.

Though I suppose we did know what happened during an exile thanks to it happening to Moony a while back. He was sent to an animal shelter. Someone could have seen him and thought, "Oh, what an adorable cat. I need to have him." And then that whole fake ownership thing would have come into play.

Thankfully, Cat rescued him from that fate.

I listened to Cat and Gloria ramble on about the next steps in their investigation as I fought sleep that came with being all warm and cozy in the sunbeam. They talked about how brave I was to find that receipt for them and about my harrowing journey to the other side of the river. They basically said I was the best cat ever, but, you know, it's not a competition.

But if it was, I would be the winner.

Just saying.

Before I knew it, I was dreaming of chasing mice down a long path in the woods, not a care in the world.

CATHERINE

"So, I'm kind of confused about something," Gloria said as we relaxed in my living room. She was making herself very comfy indeed after some sweet tea and a snack.

"What's that?" I curled up in my armchair.

"If the stream in the park empties into the Ashley River,

wouldn't the park's tributary flow *into* the Ashley? How did Kevin's body go upstream instead of down?" She said all this with her eyes closed.

"Oh, man! I didn't even think of that. That makes absolutely no sense, does it?" I sighed.

"I was picturing there being a fight on the boat, the boat turning over, and then him being unconscious and floating into the park, but it wouldn't really work like that, would it?" she asked.

"You're right. Which means he got to the park—all the way to the bridge—another way." My brain hurt from lack of sleep and trying to figure this out. "Surely his murderer didn't drag his body clear up the river?"

She opened her eyes and looked at me. "It's something to consider…"

"Oh, by the way, I sent Nathan a text," I relayed as she stretched back out on the sofa and closed her eyes again. "If I have learned anything from my sons, it's that their generation doesn't believe in talking on the phone."

"Can you imagine?" Gloria sighed. "I don't know how I would have survived adolescence without talking on the phone."

"Me either. I regularly got in trouble for hogging the phone in my house growing up!"

We both shared a laugh.

"Are you still hungry? I could make us some lunch," I offered, but when I looked over, Gloria appeared to have drifted off. She clearly needed a nap. It was good to see she wasn't superhuman after all.

She looked so peaceful lying there, the sun bouncing off her beautiful dark skin. Her head was wrapped in a zebra-print scarf today, but she was wearing plain black leggings and a jade and royal-blue striped shirt. Her shirt matched Bree's hair, come to think of it.

What did we need to figure out now? Besides the river current issue? We had the receipt and the shoe we found by the river. We really needed to know where Kevin got a boat, who was with him, how he got hit in the head and with what.

Would Nathan have the answers?

I drifted off to sleep pondering what those answers might be, and then at about two o'clock in the afternoon, my phone buzzed.

Nathan: What do you want?

Wow, that was…blunt. But I wasn't going to beat around the bush. He was just a kid; I needed to remember that. He clearly didn't have the best manners.

Me: We just want to talk to you for a few minutes. We have some questions about Kevin Morris.

Nathan: Why? You think I killed him?

The blood in my veins froze when I read that. Why would he ask that? How did he know there was foul play? That wasn't common knowledge. Bree didn't seem to know…

Me: Do you think someone killed him?

Nathan: Meet me at White Duck Tacos in Mount Pleasant in an hour.

Hmm, tacos?

I could definitely go for tacos.

But I'd let Gloria sleep a little while longer first.

"So how did you get my number?" Nathan asked before cramming half a taco in his pie-hole. Or would that be taco-hole?

"We went to pay our respects to Kevin's parents today, and Bree happened to be walking her dog right by their house when we were leaving. We asked her a few questions about Kevin, and she said you might know the answers," I explained, fork poised to dig into my nachos. They smelled amazing!

Gloria took a dainty bite of her chicken taco. "I've lived in Mount Pleasant my whole life, and I've never been in here. Thanks for recommending it."

"Yeah, it's pretty good," Nathan said. "I worked here before I got the job at Fairytale Forest. Fairytale Forest pays better."

"The Forests are good bosses," I agreed. "That's why we're asking around about Kevin's disappearance and death. Because his body was found in the park, we don't want any bad press, you know? And we don't know yet if he died of natural causes."

When I said that, Nathan paused, holding his taco just inches away from his mouth as he processed my statement. Something I said triggered him. Now I would have to figure out what it was.

"What did Bree say I might know?" he asked before

stuffing the rest of the taco in his mouth. He had now consumed one full taco, and Gloria and I had each taken three small bites. He was obviously a growing boy.

"She said you offered to go to Kevin's funeral with her," I shared.

He nodded. "I did say that. She said she'd have to get back with me."

"She also said you played that pirates game at the shop with Kevin. And that it was more than just a game—there was a club too."

He set down his second taco and stared at me. "She wasn't supposed to tell you that."

"Why not?"

"Because it's supposed to be a secret," he whispered with wide eyes before they darted around the restaurant. He was obviously wary of eavesdroppers, but there was hardly anyone around.

"Why? What kind of secret?" I demanded.

He sighed. I could tell he was struggling with the decision to tell me.

"Did you have something to do with Kevin's death?" I asked point-blank. Gloria kicked me under the table.

"Of course not!" he roared.

"Then tell me what kind of secret Kevin had. His parents obviously didn't know anything about it. And when we were at their house, we saw a receipt from Walmart that listed rope and a bunch of first-aid supplies on it. I know someone saw him at Walmart shortly before he disappeared. Was he planning for someone to get hurt? Just tell us, Nathan. We don't want anyone else to get hurt. Especially not anyone we work with."

His nostrils flared as he stared at me, obviously warring with himself on whether or not to spill his guts.

I pushed a little harder. "Bree said it was more than just a game, that there was a club. And there were initiation rites and secret fighting rituals. So it sounds like we already know quite a bit. Why don't you just fill in the blanks with what you know?"

Now he looked defeated. And he still hadn't touched his second taco. "Fine." He blew out a harsh breath. "Kevin started a secret club—a fight club. It was based on pirate lore he had researched and involved a particular fighting style that a famous pirate invented, but the basics were picked up on one of this pirate's voyages to faraway lands."

Okay, so far, this sounded crazy and made up. *Did* Kevin make it all up? What kind of research did he do? What kind of lore was he talking about?

Maybe it didn't matter. All that mattered was what happened on that boat.

"Were you a part of this club?" I pushed a bit harder.

He looked down at the napkin he was twisting in his hands. "I wanted to be, but I wasn't old enough. He said I had to be eighteen."

I sighed. "So you weren't there when it happened."

He shook his head. "No, but I knew they were going out on the boat."

"You did?" I leaned forward. "Who? Who was going out on the boat? Where did he get a boat?"

Nathan shrugged. "I don't know. He just told everyone he had one."

"Okay. But who?"

"The guys from the game at the shop." He looked away. "I don't want to get them in trouble. I don't believe they did anything wrong. And I'm not supposed to be talking about this. Everyone knows the first rule of fight club is you don't talk about it!"

"Alright, you don't have to tell us anything else. We can get the names of the other players from the game shop." I had pressed too hard. He looked nervous, and he wasn't eating anymore.

"Go ahead and eat your tacos, Nathan. I'm sorry we had to ask you some tough questions." I used one of my tortilla chips to scoop up some queso and salsa. "We're just trying to protect the park, you know? We don't want it to close down again."

"I understand." He hesitated for another moment before picking up the second taco and taking a smaller but still huge bite. He chewed thoughtfully. "I miss him, you know. I really considered him to be a mentor. He was amazing in action."

"In action?" My eyebrow rose.

"I know he came across as this really quiet guy, but he had some awesome fight moves. I went to an exhibition once where he battled his cousin Stevie, and he won. Stevie is really tall and looks strong and intimidating in all that goth gear, but Kevin kicked his butt."

"Is that so?" I shot Gloria a knowing glance. We'd already suspected Stevie might have had something to do with Kevin's disappearance because we knew he wanted to take over his role as ship captain in the pirate game.

"Yeah. Stevie always seemed jealous of him," Nathan confirmed.

"Do you think he was jealous enough to hurt his cousin?" I asked.

Nathan shoved the rest of the taco in his mouth and

considered my question as he chewed. "I don't think he'd hurt him on purpose, but he would definitely fight him with all he had."

I nodded. "Hey, we found Bree's pirate figurine in the park. Any idea how it got there?"

A sheepish grin spread across his face. "Yeah, I took it. I was hoping to give it back to her and act like I found it, but it must have fallen out of my pocket somewhere in the park on my way to Dragon's Lair. I'm glad she has it back now. I know Kevin gave it to her, and she misses him a lot."

"She really liked him, huh?"

He nodded. "Yeah, they went to school together apparently. I don't know, they're both several years older than me, but I guess they were in the same class. He had a crush on her, but he was too shy to ask her out. When he finally did, and she started playing the pirates game... Well, she saw what a great leader he was and how he wasn't actually quiet at all. I think he really grew on her."

That made me sad. "But he broke up with her?"

"Yeah. It was weird. Cassidy just started playing right in the middle of our voyage. Normally the ship captain doesn't allow newcomers to start in the middle. They have to start at the beginning. But she was Stevie's friend, and I guess Kevin felt obligated to let her join. Then next thing I knew, he dumped Bree for her. I didn't get it. He didn't seem to be her type at all, but he really was a different person when he was leading a voyage. Girls like guys who can take charge," he explained.

"Interesting. Well, maybe we should have a chat with her too," I said, and Gloria nodded in agreement.

"Oh, I have her number if you want it. She's my friend Casen's sister. I think Kevin was trying to recruit him too."

He wiped his hands on a napkin and took his phone out of his pocket.

"Okay, thanks." I took a screenshot of Cassidy's info when he pulled her up in his contacts list.

Gloria and I had both finished our lunch while he was talking about Kevin. He ate the third taco in record time as soon as he put his phone away.

"Thanks again for meeting us," I said as I stood up and gathered our trash. "Hopefully we can find some more information out from Cassidy or Stevie. If you think of anything else, will you let us know?"

"Yeah, sure." He shrugged and then gave a little smile. "I think I'm gonna go get some more tacos."

We both waved. "Bye, Nathan."

Sixteen

ZOE

When I woke up, my sunbeam was gone, and so were Cat and Gloria. They just abandoned me here? What the toe beans was that about?

I ventured into the kitchen to take a sip of water and noticed the tuna bowl was empty. I didn't remember eating it all, but who else could have indulged in some fishy goodness?

Fish...ah yes. It reminded me of the River Cats. And that in turn reminded me of my own clowder. And Snow. Were my lovelies missing me? Or had they even noticed I was gone?

When I heard the door opening, I acted on instinct, racing through the house like a streak of gray lightning and diving right under the bed. Where did that come from?

"Zoe?" I heard Cat calling me.

I sheepishly peeked out from under the bed and eventually saw a pair of biped feet moving toward me. "There you are! Are you hiding under the bed? Aw, poor thing. You're not used to being in a house, are you?"

I sauntered out, my tail waving proudly. "I was not hiding, Cat. I was merely looking for additional evidence."

"Evidence?" She laughed. "What kind of evidence are you going to find here? I didn't have anything to do with Kevin's death."

"Well, I found none, so that checks out." I sashayed into the kitchen and stood in front of the empty tuna bowl. "This bowl was once full…oh, what a blessed day that was."

"That was just a few hours ago, Zoe." She snickered as she grabbed another can of tuna out of her cupboard.

"I'm not supposed to be feeding you, you know." She opened the can and filled up my dish, and the savory aroma of tasty fish filled my senses.

Completely out of my control, my motor revved up as I ate, creating a loud purr that Cat was wildly amused by. "Oh, Zoe, try as you might, you're still just a cat, aren't you?"

I'd never tried to be anything but a cat, had I?

She was flattering herself if she thought by communicating with her, I was trying to be a biped. I had no desire to walk on two feet, wear stupid things on my body, or drink coffee. It smelled positively revolting. Not to mention all the touching humans did. It made my fur crawl just to think of it.

"Hey, I need to get back to the park," I said when I finished my tuna. "Can you take me back?"

She looked up at a round thing I knew to be a clock on her kitchen wall. Bipeds were obsessed with those things, while I was sitting here proud I didn't know how to read them.

"I dropped Gloria off at her house in Mount Pleasant,"

Cat said. "I am supposed to pick her up later tonight if I hear back from Cassidy. I also called the game shop in Charleston. I think we might head back in tonight to see if we can talk to Steve or Stevie Morris. I guess I could try to figure out how to sneak you back into the park."

"If you can get me back to the river—the correct side this time, I can squeeze through the fence," I said.

"I don't think there's a road on that side of the river, unfortunately." She smiled at me. "By the way, thanks for your help today, Zoe. We've made a lot of headway, but we still have a few more people to talk to."

I licked my paw and then used it to smooth out the fur on my cheek. "You don't need me for that, though?"

"Well, to be honest…it would be helpful to have you in the game shop. Maybe you could find another clue?"

I sighed. "Can I at least check in with my clowder first? It won't take me but a few minutes. I promise I'll be fast. I don't want them to worry about me."

Truth be told, I didn't want them taking over my leadership role like Cat and Gloria said this Stevie character took over Kevin's role in the game they played at this mythical shop.

There would be hell to pay if anyone tried to usurp my position—or if Scar pulled any more mousebrained tricks.

CATHERINE

First I went to pick up Gloria. Nothing like driving all over the Low Country on a wild goose chase, but she needed to go back to the employee parking lot to get her car. I had explained to Zoe there was no way to drop her off on the other side of the river because there was no road there.

"Then how am I getting back in?" she practically whined.

"I'm going to put you back in the bag and sneak you in. I need to find Jayden anyway. You can take care of your business while we go speak with Cassidy, and then I will pick you back up in a couple hours."

"I don't tell time, Cat."

"Oh, right. Well…hmmm." I tilted my head and drummed my fingers on my steering wheel. "Oh! You know the big clock on the tree in the middle of the park?"

"I know of it, but not how to read it," she replied.

"When the hands are straight up and down, it will be six o'clock," I told her. "That's about two hours from now. You can meet me behind the Guest Services building where I'm going to drop you off."

"Fine."

I didn't know why she was so cranky. She got spoiled today—tuna and a nap. I understood she was worried about her fellow cats, but sheesh, she had a pretty good day for a cat. And she'd gotten a heck of a lot more sleep than Gloria and I did.

"Did you get any sleep when you were at home?" I asked Gloria before dropping her off in the parking lot next to her car.

"Yes, I got a bit of a catnap," she joked, winking at Zoe, who was curled up in the backseat.

"Okay, I'll meet you at the Dunkin' in West Ashley, okay?" It wasn't too far from the park or from where Cassidy lived, and she'd agreed to speak with us at four-thirty.

"See you there!" Gloria waved as she unlocked her car and started it up.

I drove around the lot, trying to find a spot closer to the employee entrance so I didn't have to carry Zoe so far. She got heavy after a while!

"Okay, let's go." I held out the bag for her to climb into.

She gave me major attitude as she made her way inside. I didn't know why. The cats I'd known loved to sneak into bags or boxes lying around the house. Did feral cats not enjoy such things? Or was she spoiled now that she'd gotten a taste of canned tuna?

I used my ID badge to get inside, then made my way over to the Guest Services building, sneaking around back to open the bag and let her loose. "Okay, you have two hours. I'll see you right here at six, okay?"

"When the hands are straight up and down," she repeated.

"One will be up, one down," I explained.

"Gotcha."

And with that, she scampered off, leaving me holding the empty bag. I walked around to the front of the building and spotted Jayden preparing to exit the park, along with Nora and Detective Towers. "Hey!" I called, capturing their attention immediately. "Hey, I need to chat with you!" I rushed to join them as they headed toward the exits.

"I was told you were off today," Detective Towers said when I reached them.

"I am. Gloria and I have been doing some poking around

outside the park," I explained. "But I had to drop by to pick up something I left in my locker." Not exactly true but...

"I came to give Mr. Forest an update," she shared. "We searched an area across from where the park's creek empties into the Ashley River. There was evidence of a boat getting stuck in the sand, and there were some footprints that were mostly washed out with the tide and rain. We didn't really find much, but it was called in as suspicious, and since it was so close to the park, we thought we better check it out."

"If Kevin was there—outside the park," I remembered Gloria's question from earlier, "how would his body get inside the park? Wouldn't the park's creek flow down into the Ashley, not the other way around?"

"We wondered that too at first," the detective admitted. "But Mr. Forest said they have a pump there at the fence that sucks the water back up and reverses the current so there's always plenty of water in the park for the fairy ride that's over in that area. Left in its natural state, sometimes it's too shallow and exposes the boat tracks."

"I see. So, if his body got close enough to the pumps..."

"It would have sucked him into the park," she confirmed.

I cringed. That sounded terrible—but at least he didn't get sucked directly into the pumps. That would have been even more gruesome. That also explained why it was so shallow right there where it emptied into the Ashley River.

"But we didn't find any evidence he was there," she said. "What updates do you have for me?" She took out her yellow pad.

I was reluctant to share anything we'd found because we were so close to getting answers, and I didn't want the police to ruin it for us. "Oh, we were trying to figure out how Kevin ended up in the river in the first place. We had also considered a boat."

Detective Towers said, "There was definitely a boat stuck there, but we couldn't connect it to Kevin."

Jayden spoke up, "Hey, what about the mark on his forehead?"

She smiled. "Yes, we have a photo now."

"Can I see it?" I needed to go find Gloria and skedaddle so we could talk to Cassidy.

Detective Towers opened up the leather laptop bag she carried over her shoulder and retrieved a manila file folder. "Here."

I took the photo from her, which was a closeup of Kevin's forehead. It was grisly-looking, but there was a clear imprint.

And after staring at it for only a few seconds, I knew exactly what it was.

And if we were able to find the object that left that mark…we'd have our murderer.

"Got it. Sorry, I need to run. I'll call you tomorrow," I told her. "Jayden and Nora, what are you doing now?"

Jayden shrugged and turned to Nora, who very perceptively asked, "Coming with you?"

I grinned. "Let's go!"

JAYDEN, NORA, AND I EXITED INTO THE EMPLOYEE PARKING lot and practically ran to my car. Well, they ran. I just sort of walked fast, feeling the burn through my calves and feet. It had been a looooong day. And it wasn't over yet. I remembered what Gloria said earlier about dogs having four feet but only one path. We were going to take this case one step at a time until we figured out what happened to Kevin Morris.

"Where are we going?" Jayden asked as I unlocked the doors. They climbed into the back seat.

"Do you have a cat?" Nora asked. "There's a lot of hair back here."

"Just a sec." I ignored both of their questions to call Gloria. "Hey, you ready?"

"I was born ready," she said. "I'm already at Dunkin'. Just waiting on Cassidy."

"Great, be right there. And I found Jayden and Nora."

"See you soon. Be careful," was all she said before hanging up.

I threw my Rogue into drive and carefully backed out of my parking space, then I hightailed it over to the Dunkin' on 17 in West Ashley. I parked bedside Gloria, and we all hopped out.

"You think Cassidy is involved in this?" Jayden asked after I caught them up on what we'd found out on the way here.

"Not the fight club," I answered. "But I think she knows something."

"She mentioned Kevin in past tense," Nora remembered. "Like he wasn't still around—this was before his body was found."

"I noticed that too," I shared. "Okay, let's see if she's inside with Gloria."

I spotted Gloria at a booth in the back and recognized Cassidy's hair from behind. My entourage and I approached. "Hey, let's move this party to a table," I suggested, gesturing toward a bigger space across the way.

We all moved and settled into new seats. "Hi, Cassidy. I'm Cat. You remember Jayden and Nora from The Wizard's Spell?"

"I knew you guys weren't real P 'n P players. My cousin was suspicious of you too," she scoffed.

"How are you and Stevie related?" I asked.

"My mom and his mom are sisters," she clarified.

That was interesting—she was related to him on the other side of the family as Kevin. I supposed it was alright for her and Kevin to date, then, though why and how were still somewhat of a mystery to me.

"We just want to figure out what happened to Kevin," Jayden explained. "And we were gathering some information that night. That was before his body was found. Now we want to figure out if someone is responsible for his death."

At that, Cassidy's eyes lowered to the table, where she fidgeted with an opal ring on her pinky finger. "Well, I don't know anything about that."

"Do you know about the secret fight club Kevin ran?" I cut right to the chase. I wanted as much information as possible before I confronted her cousin about it. He was next on my list.

"I really didn't know Kevin that well," she said quietly.

"Didn't he dump his girlfriend Bree for you?" I challenged her. "It seems like he wouldn't have done that if he didn't think you guys were in a relationship."

Her nostrils flared as she seemed to consider her response carefully. "My cousin—who is also his cousin on the other side of the family—introduced us. He...encouraged me to go out with him."

"So you did date him?" Nora was getting into this as well, leaning forward in her seat, eyes trained on Cassidy.

"We went out a few times," she admitted, "but it wasn't serious. I'm sorry he broke up with Bree—I never asked him to do that. She seemed like a nice girl. But from what I understand, she wasn't supportive of his...club."

"How much do you know about this club?" I asked.

"I just know that you had to fight him to get inducted into it. He ran some training sessions for pledges to practice. It was some weird fighting style that I think he made up, but Steve said he learned it doing research on pirates."

"Was your cousin Stevie part of the club?" I asked.

She rolled her eyes. "Yeah, I mean, I guess so."

I pinned her with a penetrating stare. "What do you mean by that?"

She blew out a breath. "I think the whole thing is stupid, and I didn't really want anything to do with it. I told my mom about it, and she told my aunt. Kevin was mad because I wasn't supposed to tell anyone. It was supposed to be a secret."

Interesting. We were sort of getting somewhere. We needed to talk to Cousin Stevie. He and Kevin might have fought about his mom finding out....

"Do you know anything about your cousin wanting to take over Kevin's ship captain role in the Prisons & Pirates game?" I questioned.

"I mean, it was pretty common knowledge that he wanted to be the ship captain, but his dad wouldn't let him. Kevin—well, he didn't go by Kevin at the shop. He went by The Silver Dagger—he brought in a lot of business for

Uncle Steve. He was really good at the game. He acted stuff out. He had a big personality there. You'd never know it by spending time with him as Kevin. He was quiet and shy. He wouldn't even kiss me." She rolled her eyes here.

"It sounds like he was a charismatic leader," I summarized.

"Yeah, you could say he had the rizz." She shrugged. "But only when he was The Silver Dagger."

I glanced at Jayden and Nora for a translation, and they only smiled.

"Do you know anything about his disappearance? What might have happened that night?"

She shook her head. "Nope. I don't know anything."

"You're sure," I checked.

"Yeah, they don't let females into their little club," she maintained.

Why did I feel like she was lying?

"If you think of anything that may help us, can you let us know? I think we're going to go talk to your cousin now," I explained.

She nodded. "Okay, I will." She got up and took two steps away from the table before she whipped back around. "Kevin was a nice guy. He really didn't deserve what happened to him."

Seventeen

Cat said I had two hours. I wasn't sure exactly how long that was, but I knew it wasn't a terribly long stretch of time, and I didn't want to let her down. She just basically saved my life today, after all.

However, I did almost die, and there were a few cats responsible for that. Naturally, I intended to make them pay. And I had a good idea of how to do it.

I was going to humiliate Scar and give him an experience he would never forget. If it worked out the way I hoped, it might even get him removed from the park.

Paws crossed.

First, I had to round up the troops. It was broad daylight, so I'd have to be super stealthy. I raced behind the buildings on the main street of the park, avoiding bipeds snacking on popcorn, slurping ice cream and carrying large balloons. As soon as I got to the courtyard, I snuck under the labyrinth of bushes to where my clowder called home.

Those lazy felines were all napping, as they typically did during this time of day when the sun was starting its descent, but it was still quite warm. I heard the distant rumble of thunder and wondered if a rain shower might factor into my plans. That would make it all the better!

Snow was asleep in a white ball with his ringed tail wrapped behind him. I nudged him awake, and his blue eyes slowly blinked open.

"Zoe!" His mouth spread into an almost-smile. "Where've you been? We didn't know if you made it, to be honest."

"I see you didn't come looking for me," I snarled back to him.

"We had our hands full with those thugs that were harassing you," he reminded me. "We successfully chased them back into their own territory thanks to the help from your River Cat friends."

I definitely owed them one, but they were going to enjoy seeing this little demonstration too—and it would play out right in front of them. "Yes, speaking of which, I have a plan to exact revenge on Scar and his thugs, and I need your help."

He rubbed his paws together. "That sounds delightful!"

I carefully explained what I needed him to do. It involved rounding up Moony and the rest of the Courtyard Clowder, then heading over to the River Cats territory and giving them some very specific instructions.

"And we have to hurry," I warned him. "I don't have much time to complete this before my biped friends come back to pick me up. I'm still helping them avenge the death of your...landlord, for lack of a better term."

"Got it." He stood up and stretched as he yawned,

showing off his gleaming white teeth. Then he sat regally, showing off his commanding presence and those piercing blue eyes. "I'm on it."

"See you there!" I tossed over my shoulder as I ran so fast, I was merely a gray blur. I was about to set the next part of my plan in motion.

"Vinny!" I called when I neared Scar's territory. "Oh, Vinny!"

I could barely contain my excitement, I was so ready to see this plan come to fruition. Fortunately, Scar's dominion was in a quieter part of the park, and there weren't any bipeds nearby since it wasn't near any major attractions or eateries.

Unfortunately, Vinny didn't appear. It was Gil and Frank, two of his thugs.

"What do you want, Z?" Frank sneered.

"I need to talk to Vinny please." I forced the words to come out as sweetly as possible, like they were dipped in honey.

"Haven't you done enough? Vinny is still recovering from that stunt your cronies pulled last night," Gil said.

"Well, that's why I'm here," I cooed. "I've come to apologize."

I had no sooner gotten the words out of my mouth than a black and white head popped up from behind a trash can. "Did you say apologize?" Vinny sauntered out, but he had a limp. He'd clearly gotten hurt in the rumble the night before. Served him right.

"Yeah, I feel really bad about my friends ambushing you, and we want to make it up to you and Scar." I walked in a circle and then plopped down, trying to look all contrite and innocent.

"Make it up to us how?" Vinny's curiosity was definitely piqued as he paced around me, giving me a sniff.

"Well, the River Cats wanted to show you some hospitality, and they've put together a fish feast for you and Scar to enjoy," I said.

"A feast?" I had Gil and Frank's attention too.

"Yes, and a couple other surprises. Can you get Scar? I want to personally apologize to him and tell him what we're prepared to do to make amends." I was really laying it on thick.

"Well, Z, I never thought I'd see the day," Vinny said, the words oozing out of him like pus from a festering wound.

I tried to keep my pleasant demeanor and not cringe as he moved so close to me, his whiskers were touching mine. "You want me to go get Scar now?"

"Yes, please. I know how much he loves fish. They're catching them right now, so if we don't get a move on, they're going to stink."

"It's the middle of the park day, Z," Vinny said. "You know Scar doesn't like to go out in the daytime."

Scar didn't like to go out ever. That was why this plan was so brilliant.

"I know that, but right now is the best fishing, according to the River Cats. They want it to be fresh, and they're preparing a special treat for both of you." I looked up at the sky. The clouds were gathering, thickening, darkening. I crossed my paws that the timing would be as good as I wanted it to be.

Vinny considered my offer for a moment, and then Frank piped up: "I'll go in Scar's place, Vin. Fresh fish sounds mighty tasty, and you know we haven't had a good meal in a while."

Scar chose his clowder's territory poorly. Because it wasn't near the main attractions or restaurants, prey was scarcer here. Not to mention the fact that they regularly overhunted and depleted the supply. No wonder they were always trying to infiltrate other clowders' territories.

"You're not getting Scar's surprise," Vinny snapped before limping back over to me. "Fine. We'll get him. Frank, Gil, tell Alfie to bring Scar out here."

The two rushed off to do their master's bidding, and I just sat primly, biding my time.

"This better be legit, Z, and not a scam of some sort. Because if it is, then you guys are gonna regret it."

"Why would we try to scam you?" I asked sweetly. The words tasted foul on my sandpaper tongue.

"Because you hate us!" he fired back.

I didn't have to answer because Gil and Frank reappeared with Scar right between them. I hadn't seen him in a while. He looked old and frail, like his bones were creaking with every movement. He looked even worse than Mr. Cool Cat.

"What's this about, Z?" he asked in his crotchety old-man voice.

"We put together a surprise for you. We felt bad that a few of your cats got injured last night in the brawl down by the river. The River Cats wanted to make it up to you. I'm their ambassador." I gave a little bow like I saw a biped do once on some show we watched in the security office.

"What do we have to do?" Vinny asked.

"Follow me!"

I led them all through the park, ducking under benches and behind trash cans, traipsing through the flora and even through a special maintenance corridor that ran on one side of the go-kart track. That led us right to the river.

"How are we gonna get across it without anyone seeing us?" Vinny asked. "There are a ton of bipeds around."

There were bipeds on the bridge, and a long queue of bipeds waiting to get into the Water Fairy Adventure ride. But I had a plan. And a secret.

"It's part of the surprise," I said. "You'll have to follow the sound of my voice because it's going to be dark where we're going."

"We're cats. We can see in the dark. Duh," Vinny snapped.

"Oh, you have to do it with your eyes closed. Sorry— those are the rules the River Cats have. They'll be leading you the rest of the way."

We were in the marshy area next to the river, where the cattails were so high, we were easily concealed. Delta was nearby—I could smell her. And she knew to make an appearance as soon as she heard me call out "River Cats."

"Hi, Scar and Vinny. Nice to officially meet you." She dipped her chin in acknowledgment. "We have a special treat for two special cats. It's an honor for me to share this with you."

Vinny and Scar looked at each other, obviously charmed by Delta and her striking tortoiseshell beauty and smooth voice. "Lead the way," Scar said.

Anticipation raced through me as I bolted ahead down the secret tunnel that went under the river to the other side, right where the boats for the Water Fairy Adventure rounded the bend after leaving the dock where they departed. I never knew this tunnel existed until Delta and her cohorts showed it to me.

As I exited the tunnel, I heard the first crack of lightning and boom of thunder. *Oh, yes! I love it when a plan comes together.* I spotted Snow, Moony, and the rest of my clowder hanging out behind the Water Fairy Adventure building, out of sight of bipeds. Everyone was gathered for the show.

I had given Snow detailed instructions, and he met Delta on the other side, guiding Scar and Vinny to the River Bank. "Just jump when I tell you to jump," Snow said. "But keep your eyes closed until you land. Otherwise, the surprise won't work."

It was a good thing Scar and his thugs were severely lacking in common sense, or this would never have worked. But I'd known them almost my whole life, and it became apparent early on that they weren't the sharpest claws on the paw. I crept out of the tunnel so I could have a better view, but I kept myself hidden in the reeds.

Snow waited for the boat to lurch to a stop. That meant a new set of boats was being loaded at the dock. "Jump!" he yelled.

Just as I saw Scar and Vinny sail through the air and into the cat fairy boat, the skies opened up and rain cascaded down.

Vinny let out a loud screech as he landed and the rain began to pelt his coat. Scar looked up at Snow with a scowl. "Where's the fish?" he demanded.

"Up at the top!" Snow shouted back over the downpour.

Vinny lifted his nose, smelling, and leapt up to the bow where the cat fairy figurehead proudly guided the boat. On the little perch where Snow and I had leapt to the walkway inside the ride just a few nights ago were two small fish. Vinny and Scar weren't going to let those fish go to waste, so they made their way out onto the little ledge, their bodies shivering and their fur matting with the rain.

And then the boat began to move again, forming a parade in a long line of boats leaving the dock. As bipeds on the bridge and in the open queue began to unfurl umbrellas or cover themselves with plastic ponchos, the cat fairy boat proudly sailed toward the bridge.

I heard the first biped shout and point at the cat fairy boat with the two soaked cats sitting on top of the figurehead. Soon, the entire bridge full of bipeds was laughing and pointing.

It was the most glorious sight I'd ever seen!

Then I realized I might be running late to meet Cat. I raced through the secret tunnel to the other side of the river. The park guests were so concerned with trying to stay dry, no one noticed me sprint to the courtyard, where I saw one hand pointing up and one pointing down on the tree.

It was time to meet Cat, but the image of Scar and Vinny, soaked to their bones, on top of the cat fairy boat as they ate their measly little fish and created a spectacle the park guests wouldn't soon forget would stay with me for the rest of my life.

Eighteen

"Holy smokes, you're soaked!" I held out the bag so Zoe could step in. "I think I have a towel in the car."

"Thanks, hadn't noticed," she snarked back at me as I scooped up the bag and rushed back out the exit. My car was conveniently located so we didn't get too much wetter. I let the cat out of the bag—*see what I did there?*—in the back seat as I rummaged through the junk in the very back for a towel.

She actually allowed me to dry her off. She must have been pretty miserable. Poor thing—she'd nearly drowned last night, and now she was soaking wet again.

"Gloria, Jayden and Nora went to the game store where Kevin played his game—the one owned by his uncle," I explained. "It's looking like his cousin might have been the one who hit him, but if he isn't, he probably knows who did.

We're looking for a specific object—that's what we need your help with."

"What is it?" she asked.

"Remember the tattoo you saw on Kevin's back?"

"Yes?"

"We're looking for the real version of that—a dagger with a skull and crossbones on the handle. We found the mini keychain version in the river, but there must be a big version. The mark on Kevin's face where he was hit looks like it could have been made with the handle of a dagger like that. I could be wrong—but it makes as much sense as anything else."

"And you think the murderer might still have the weapon?" she pondered.

"I think it's possible." I tossed the towel down beside her then climbed into the driver's seat. Before I had a chance to back out of the parking spot, I got a text from Jayden.

Jayden: We went to the store, but neither Steve nor Stevie is there tonight. The dumb kid working there actually gave me their home address. Apparently Stevie still lives with his parents.

Me: Awesome! Text it to me, and I'll meet you there.

Jayden: They're apparently at their beach house on Isle of Palms.

Me: Haven't been over there in a coon's age. See ya there!

Isle of Palms was home to some very expensive, very

swanky properties. "Looks like we're headed back over the Ravenel Bridge, Zoe."

"Yeah, whatever."

It was clear she didn't share my affinity for bridges. "It's about a thirty-minute drive, so sit tight or feel free to take a snooze."

"I don't need your permission to do that, but thank you."

Boy, she was a snarky little thing tonight, wasn't she? *Wet cats, sheesh!*

Hopefully she'd dry out before we reached our destination, though with the wind whipping my Rogue around on the road and rain falling in sheets across my windshield, I didn't know if we would be able to avoid getting wet all over again when we reached our destination.

I'd just have to cross my fingers and hope this trip would be worth our efforts.

I PULLED IN BEHIND GLORIA'S CAR, AND THERE WAS ANOTHER car in the driveway too. Judging by the mermaid and Barbie bumper stickers and the age and disrepair of the vehicle, I didn't imagine it could possibly belong to Stevie or his father. I wondered if they already had company.

"Eeep!" Nora screeched when she watched me pluck Zoe out of the back seat and into the shopping bag.

Oh, yeah. Jayden and Nora are here...

"I saw the cat hair in your car!" Nora cooed. "So you *do* have a cat!"

"Wait, is that Zoe? From the park?" Jayden questioned.

Gloria shot me a nervous look, and I stammered, "Shh… please don't say anything…"

Jayden pretended to zip his lips and throw away the key, like we used to do when we were kids. I didn't know people still did that, but it was adorable. Nora giggled and mirrored him, making the same gesture.

These were two good kids, ones I was proud to have on our team. Now they were going to help us solve this case. All we had to do was get Stevie to admit to hitting his cousin and then leaving him to drown when the boat capsized—if that was indeed what happened.

And hopefully we'd figure out where they got the boat and what happened to said boat as well.

"Well, are we ready to go in?" I glanced around at my crew: Gloria, Jayden and Nora, and I patted Zoe in the bag.

"Hey, look at that." Jayden pointed to the attached garage. On the other side of it was a tall carport—only it didn't have a car inside it—it had a boat.

"That can't be the boat they were in though." I shook my head. "Snow said it was wooden—said he floated on a piece of wood after the boat capsized."

I heard Zoe say something like, "You can't believe everything Snow says. He's full of it."

"Who's Snow?" Jayden asked.

"Uh…never mind. They have a boat. Good to know." I smiled and looked up at the sky. "Looks like it's going to start raining again. Let's get inside." We had been enjoying a brief reprieve from the rain, but I knew it wouldn't last, and the sun had already checked out for the night. The sky made it look way past six-forty-five, but that was what time it was, according to my watch.

We made our way onto the beautiful wide porch decked

out with enormous planters on either side of the door, and Gloria rang the doorbell. It was one of those fancy double doors with glass panels on either side, so we saw a figure approach before the door swung open to reveal someone unexpected.

"Cassidy," I said. "Didn't expect you here."

"Well, you said you wanted to talk to my cousin, so I thought I'd give him a heads-up. My aunt and uncle aren't here," she said.

"But Stevie is?" I questioned.

She crossed her arms over her chest. "Yeah. Waiting for y'all to show up."

"Well, we're ready to talk to him." I glanced around at my crew, and they all nodded and murmured affirmatively.

She stepped aside and opened one of the doors, allowing us to enter the massive beach house. We were right on the ocean, and with the storm riling up the waves, I could hear them crashing on the beach just a few yards away.

Cassidy led us through to the living room, which was full of pristine ivory leather furniture. This was really just the Morrises' beach house? They had another house somewhere else? They could afford two houses on what he made at the game shop? Impressive.

"My aunt's a cardiologist," Cassidy explained, seeming to read my mind.

"Oh, okay." Well, that made more sense.

"And both of my grandparents were doctors too," she continued. "This was their beach house."

Alrighty then. Generational wealth for the win.

"This is a lovely home, Stevie," I greeted the young man, who was sprawled out on one of the sofas facing the back wall of the house, which was made up entirely of windows.

The sea looked angry, pounding against the sand with a vengeance. I set my shopping bag down behind one of the couches, letting Zoe roam off to do her job.

We were at the beach house, but I didn't know where Stevie resided most of the time. Was it here or at their other residence? She might not find the dagger if Stevie wasn't currently living here.

I was trying not to get my hopes up too high, but that dagger was a symbol of his rivalry with his cousin. He'd want to keep it as a trophy. A testament to his victory over his cousin.

How sad.

"Can we chat with you a second?" I tried again to get his attention.

Cassidy plopped down next to him. "C'mon, Cuz, tell these nice people how much you miss your cousin Kevin."

I rolled my eyes. He was going to put on an act for us? Great. We just needed some food—then we could have dinner and a show.

We all made ourselves comfortable as Cassidy tried to coax Stevie into sitting up and talking to us. She whispered something in his ear we couldn't hear, and he finally repositioned himself as if his body was made of lead.

"What do you want?" he snarled, but it seemed like it was taking all his effort to do so.

"We want to know what happened to your cousin Kevin." I laced my fingers together, trying to rein in my anger. I'd try to be respectful, but I was sure his abject grief was all an act.

"He's dead." Stevie's gaze was focused on the sea roiling under the thick layers of clouds.

"How did he die?" I asked.

Stevie shrugged but still didn't make eye contact with any of us. "I don't know exactly. They found his body in a river at the amusement park where y'all work."

"He was hit in the head with an object," I noted. "Do you have any idea what kind of object may have hit him?"

"I wasn't there," Stevie insisted.

"Do you own a boat?" I asked.

"My parents do." His gaze flicked over to me for a fraction of a second before it shot back to the window.

"Can you tell me a little about the secret club Kevin started? The one about pirates?" I knew this was going to be difficult, but I thought he'd want to exonerate himself, even if it meant lying to us. He just seemed so defeated. So depressed.

Maybe it was regret?

At my question, he slumped forward, resting his elbows on his knees as his head hung down. He was wearing all black again today—black skinny jeans with chains and a black Bauhaus t-shirt. His pale skin looked almost gray, sicklier than it had at the game store when we saw him last week.

"I don't wanna talk about it."

Cassidy put her hand on his knee. "Come on, Cuz. These people just want to get to the truth. They're helping the police. They want to find Kevin's killer."

His head shot up. "How do you know he was killed? Maybe he just drowned."

That was more like what I was expecting.

"We know he was hit in the head with an object, and we think it was a dagger with a skull and crossbones on the handle. It likely matches the large tattoo Kevin had on his back. Do you know anything about that? Have you ever seen him with a dagger like that?"

"Okay. Fine." Stevie scrubbed his hands down his face. "I'll tell you what I know."

Finally! I glanced over at Jayden, Nora and Gloria, and they all seemed to be hanging on the edges of their seats.

"Kevin did start a...gathering. A crew, he called it," Stevie said, sitting up straighter on the sofa.

His features had become more open. Maybe he was ready to confess? I was going to have to be crafty in coaxing the confession from him.

"How long ago was that?" I asked to keep him talking.

Stevie huffed out a long breath. "I think Kevin was always fascinated with pirates. When we were little we went to the dungeon—the one in the historic district near Rainbow Row, you know it?"

We all nodded.

"They did some sort of pirate night when we were kids. You dressed up like a pirate, and they had games and story time. They told a bunch of stories about pirates who had been locked up in that dungeon. And we got these plastic swords to play with. Kevin was obsessed with it. He started to collect pirate stuff. And he read books on them. He was like a walking encyclopedia of pirate knowledge. He knew all about their weapons and discovered this unique fighting style pirates of the Black Sea used.

"Then a few years ago when he was in college, he started playing the Prisons & Pirates game. Well, obviously he was into it. He played it in Columbia, up in Charlotte, and in Atlanta, and then he brought it here to Charleston. He was the first ship captain in the area, and of course my dad was happy to host his games at his store.

It brought in a lot of customers, and my dad stocked a lot of products for the game, the figurines and the maps and stuff.

"Kevin was a totally different person when he was talking about pirates or playing P 'n P. He wanted to be called his ship captain name—The Silver Dagger—all the time. And then, a couple of years ago, he started to form this secret crew. He called it the Cutlass Crew. We had to learn the Black Sea pirate fighting style and learn to swordfight with cutlasses. He had cat o'nine tails and daggers and all sorts of stuff he'd collected through the years. To be initiated, you had to fight him. You had to draw blood before he did. Hardly anyone could, but it didn't stop people from trying."

I stopped him for a moment, fascinated by the extremes Kevin went to for this pirate obsession, to live in this sort of alternative universe where he was a ship captain, and he had his own crew. "So who was part of this crew? Were you?"

He nodded. "Yeah, me and a couple guys Kevin worked with. And a couple guys from P 'n P night at the store. A few guys weren't initiated, just running around with us, but they couldn't be official until they fought him and won. He regularly held training. And we did some other weird stuff—I won't go into the details—"

"So how many people total knew about this secret club?" I asked.

He started to count on his fingers. "Well, like six or seven of us. Until Cassidy found out."

Cassidy closed her eyes and looked down at her hand, which was still on Stevie's knee.

"One of Kevin's rules was no wenches. And you had to be eighteen. So his girlfriend Bree couldn't join, and neither could this kid she worked with named Nathan, who was really jazzed about it."

Ah yes, Nathan.

"So how did Cassidy find out about it?" I asked.

Cassidy took over the conversation now, "Kevin just told me about it. Like, I think he thought it would make me like him more." She rolled her eyes. "I thought the whole thing was dumb, and I didn't want to go out with him anyway."

Stevie reached out and gave her a smack on the arm.

"Hey!" she squealed. "I wouldn't have ever gotten involved in this mess if it wasn't for you."

"What do you mean by that, Cassidy?" I questioned.

"Yeah, what *do* you mean by that?" Stevie pressed, turning to face her.

"Since we're confessing..." Her nostrils flared as she stared at her cousin, and he glared back at her as if daring her to keep talking. "Stevie wanted me to go out with Kevin so he could ask Bree out."

"Is that so?" My eyes widened as I took in the two of them, wondering if I could believe Cassidy's accusation. "Bree didn't say anything about you at all."

"That's because I haven't asked her out yet. I was waiting for all this to blow over—"

"So you had a pretty strong motive to get rid of your cousin," I noted. "One, you wanted his girlfriend. Two, you wanted his spot at the head of the P 'n P table. Maybe you wanted to take over his secret fight club too?"

"No!" Stevie protested. "I would never have hurt him—except for the initiation fight when I had to. But he asked for it! That was part of the game!"

"Is that what happened the night he disappeared?" Was the whole thing an accident, and Kevin died playing the game he himself had created? But that didn't explain how he got hit in the head…

"No…I was initiated like two years ago, when he first started it." He blew out another breath and looked at Cassidy again.

"Do either of you know what happened that night?" I asked them. "Because I have a feeling one of you know. Where's the dagger with the skull and crossbones?" I scanned the living room, looking for Zoe. Did she drag it in here while we were talking?

I looked on the other side of the sofa where I'd left the bag with her in it, and there was a muddy shoe. Just one shoe.

I picked it up and turned it over in my hand, suddenly jogging my memory. *See what I did there?*

"Is this your shoe?" It was a match to the one we found near the river.

Stevie shook his head. "No, I only wear black boots. Not sneakers." He looked offended I would even suggest he might wear a fancy-looking white sneaker.

And then…

I realized where I'd seen those shoes before.

Nineteen

CATHERINE

"Where's your dad?" was my next question.

Stevie straightened tall against the sofa. "I don't know, why?"

I was still holding the shoe as if it might suddenly disappear if I set it down. "Can you get ahold of him?"

"Why?" he demanded.

"We need to speak with him." I glanced around the room at my team. They probably had no idea the connection I'd just made, but this was a breakthrough, and we needed answers stat.

Stevie rolled his eyes. "I'll text him and find out where he is." He pulled his phone out of one of the many pockets in his pants and fired off a text.

He received a reply almost immediately. "Oh, he's on his way back here…with pizza."

"Guess we're gonna be having a pizza party then." I

gestured to Jayden. "Can I speak with you for a second in another room?"

Cassidy stood up too. "So you guys are staying for dinner? I'll get things ready in the kitchen."

"We don't want to intrude on your dinner, but we do need to speak with Steve Senior," I explained as I pointed toward a hallway that probably led to bedrooms. Jayden followed me.

"What's up? Why do you need to talk to his dad?" Jayden asked. "You're not buying his story?"

"That shoe—we found another one just like it where the river in Fairytale Forest meets the Ashley. Do you know anything about the brand? Is it common?"

"YOLOs? They're super pricey. Several hundred dollars. My parents won't even get me a pair." He rolled his eyes.

"Okay. Here's what I want you to do: call Detective Towers, tell her we've had a breakthrough in the case and give her this address. Tell her to bring backup."

"Are you sure?" He stared at me with wide brown eyes.

I nodded. "Yeah. But we still need that dagger. I'm assuming Zoe didn't find it."

He blinked. "What do you mean?"

"Zoe brought me the shoe," I explained. "But I told her to look for the dagger."

He just continued to blink.

I sighed. "Look, I'm going to tell you a secret, but you have to promise not to tell anyone, and especially not your parents."

He looked mildly excited by that idea. "What is it?"

"Zoe helped me solve the Heather Suka case by finding evidence. Couldn't have solved the case without her. She's helping with this case too."

"She is? How do you—?" He seemed too stunned to finish his sentence.

"Don't worry about all that. What I want you to do is go see if you can find the dagger. You know what we're looking for, right? Like a long knife with a handle that has a skull and crossbones on it, like a separate piece that has been welded on, probably made of metal as well."

"Got it. I'll see what I can do."

"Check Stevie's room if you can find it…and his parents'. And if there's a den or anything like that."

"I will." He gave me a businesslike nod and took off down the hall.

I went back to the living room and sat down next to Gloria. "Is everything okay?" she asked me.

"Yep. Just waiting to talk to Mr. Morris." I winked at Stevie, who was still sitting in the same spot. Cassidy had gone into the kitchen, and I could hear her clattering around in there, gathering plates and utensils and setting the table in the dining room.

Darkness had settled over Isle of Palms, and I could no longer tell if the storm was raging. Would Steve Morris show up first or Detective Towers? Only time would tell.

Twenty minutes later, there was a grinding sound, and Stevie stood up. "That's the garage. My dad is home."

We all stood up, though I wasn't sure why. For some reason, following Stevie to the back door to greet his father just sort of happened. He was carrying three pizza boxes, so it was just as well we were there to help.

"Who are all those people?" He glanced around, not really meeting any of our eyes.

"Some friends from P 'n P," his son said—not entirely a lie?

"Hi, Uncle Steve," Cassidy said sweetly. "I set the table in the dining room."

"Great, let's put these pizzas on the buffet in there." He handed one to his son.

The aroma of mozzarella, green peppers and pepperoni filled the air, and my stomach rumbled. Did I even eat today? It had been a crazy day. It felt like it had been going on forever. Oh, yeah, I had nachos when we met with Nathan. That seemed like it happened last week!

While everyone settled in the dining room, I went back into the living room to check on Zoe. "You did good, Zoe. You might have broken the case."

"Well, I did my best, but I didn't see the dagger you spoke of. This shoe, though, it smelled like the one we found at the river."

"I'm sure it's a match," I assured her, smiling. "Can you hang in here just a little longer while we talk to Mr. Morris? I'll get you whatever you want to eat afterwards."

"Fine. I don't see as I have much of a choice." She curled back down in the bag and closed her eyes.

"Were you talking to the cat?"

I heard the voice and whipped around to spot Jayden standing in the hallway where it met the living room. *Oops!* Guess there was no way to hide it now.

"Oh, everyone talks to their pets, don't they?" I shrugged.

"But Zoe isn't your pet," he insisted. "Can you really talk to her? Does she talk back?"

Before I could ask him if he found the dagger, I heard Gloria call, "Cat, you need to come in here now!"

My heart started to pound as my feet kicked into gear. Jayden beat me to the dining room, but not by much.

"Y'all were at my shop last week." It sounded like an accusation. "And you—" Steve pointed at me, "—you bought a game for your son. What do you people want?"

"Well, I have a question for you," I said as pleasantly as possible "Do you mind if we sit down? We can chat while you enjoy your pizza."

He rolled his eyes. "That's mighty kind of you." He looked around the room at Gloria, Jayden and Nora. "There's enough pizza for everyone, so you might as well join us. Drinks in the fridge."

So...the guy I'm about to question regarding his nephew's murder is offering to feed us dinner.

Awkward!

"We couldn't," I insisted, earning scowls from Jayden and Nora, but the biggest scowl of all was on Gloria's face. "We won't take up much of your time. I just have a question—"

"What's that?" He put two pieces of pepperoni, onion and green pepper pizza on his plate and sat at the head of the table.

I took a seat next to him and settled myself before asking, "Do you wear YOLO shoes?"

He looked down at his feet. "Yeah. Just got this pair actually."

They were the same pair he was wearing in the game shop the night I bought the game for my son. They were exactly the same as the muddy ones we had found, only clean and brand-new.

"Interesting." I smiled. "Do you think a lot of people wear the same style?"

He laughed. "No—these are custom-made. The guy who invented YOLOs actually went to college with me. Nobody else owns a pair exactly like these. He made them especially for me." He seemed very proud of this fact.

"Oh, I see. You said you just got a new pair. So these are the only ones in the world like them?" I was biding my time before going in for the kill—so to speak.

He took a bite of pizza and chewed carefully for a moment. "You seem awfully interested in my shoes. You can buy regular YOLOs in higher-end shoe stores. But this particular pair is custom-made. The only other ones like it are the ones I had before it. But I got them muddy—actually lost one of them."

"How did you get them muddy?" I liked where this was going.

"Well, funny story, I found out Stevie here had taken my boat for some stupid club he was in, and he didn't ask, so I was pretty angry when my niece Cassidy told me what he did." He shot a smile at Cassidy across the table from him, but she frowned back. "So I went to go find him and get my boat back."

Wow, Cassidy was quite a snitch, wasn't she?

"He took your boat? The one here at this house?" I questioned.

"Yeah, he was trying to take it up the Ashley River for some reason. A stupid hairbrained idea of his cousin's, no doubt. When Cassidy told her mom what he and Kevin were up to, and then she told my wife, I was livid. The entire thing is so idiotic. Kevin started a cult and got my son involved. And then he stole my boat!"

"Kevin stole your boat?" I clarified.

"Well, Stevie took it, but only because Kevin forced him to. The power he had over my son was—"

I saw the frown on Cassidy's face deepen as she and Stevie exchanged a look.

"So you found them on the Ashley River and demanded your boat back?" I asked.

Steve set down his pizza. I'd apparently reinvigorated his anger from that night because his face turned red, and his eyes narrowed as deep lines etched in his forehead and a vein throbbed in his neck. "When I found the two of them in my boat, stuck in the shallows—that was the last straw. I told him he was done playing his stupid pirate game at my shop, and that Stevie was done hanging out with him and doing this stupid secret pirate stuff. I sent Stevie home in my truck and told Kevin I was taking my boat back. That he was on his own for finding a way back home."

"And how did that go over?" My heart started to pound in my chest as we grew ever closer to the answers we'd been seeking.

"Well, he was mad. He lunged at me with some stupid weapon, and I easily disarmed him. Then he hauled off and punched me in the gut. I was so angry, I threw his cat overboard, and then he was as mad as a hornet. While wrestling the dagger away from me, he ended up in the river."

He ended up in the river. No mention of hitting him with the dagger handle.

"And then what happened?" I glanced at the faces around the table, and it looked like everyone was holding their breath.

"Nothing. I took my boat and went home." He shrugged and picked up his pizza again.

"So Kevin just disappeared after that. And you didn't think anything of it?" I couldn't believe he was confessing to leaving his nephew for dead. "You know his body was found in the park just up the river from where you confronted them in the boat, right?"

"Well, he was alive when we left, wasn't he, Stevie?" He glared at his son.

Who said nothing. *Didn't Steve just say he sent his son home in his truck?*

Just as I was about to ask him about the dagger and the mark on Kevin's face, the doorbell rang.

Detective Towers.

"Excuse me." Steve threw down his napkin and headed toward the door.

No one said a word.

Then Jayden held up his phone and waved it. I saw he was recording the entire conversation.

Oh my.

Shouts erupted from the foyer, so we all raced in there to see Steve had started arguing with Detective Towers and the uniformed officer she brought for backup.

"I didn't do anything wrong!" he shouted. "Everyone get out of my house! Now!"

I said to Steve's back, "You hit Kevin in the head with the handle of the dagger, didn't you? You knocked him out cold and dumped his body overboard. That's what really happened, isn't it?"

Stevie yelled, tears streaming down his face, "Did you kill him, Dad? You killed Kevin? You told me he must have drowned after you left!"

Steve whipped around. "I don't know what you're

talking about. He wrestled the dagger away from me. He could have stabbed me with that thing!"

Jayden stepped forward. "Do you mean this dagger?" He slid it out of the pocket of his cargo shorts. "The one that has blood on it?" He held it up, and I could see reddish-brown splotches around the eye sockets of the skull.

Gloria and Nora gasped. Detective Towers calmly reached into her bag and pulled out a plastic evidence sleeve. "You can put that right in here, Jayden."

Then Steve pushed his way past Jayden, the detective, and the officer and made a break for it.

"It's an island—not sure where he thinks he's going!" I said as Detective Towers and the officer sprinted after him.

We stepped out onto the porch to watch the chase. Which ended up pretty anticlimactic since the officer tackled him at the end of his driveway.

Guess those fancy custom-made YOLOs didn't help him run very fast.

Twenty

ZOE

It was nice to be home. Cat snuck me into work with her the next day after our tour of the Low Country. She wasn't on the schedule, but she needed to speak with the owners about Kevin's murder. And I guess it did end up being a murder since Kevin's uncle Steve admitted to bludgeoning him with the dagger handle and then leaving him for dead in the water. And he lost his fancy shoe while trying to get his boat unstuck so he could make his getaway.

I always hoped I'd have the occasion to use the word "bludgeoning," but now that I'd used it, it felt kind of sour. But it was nothing a couple of tasty mice couldn't fix.

"Well, the gang's all back together," Ziti purred as I gathered my clowder around me.

"I now understand why bipeds say difficult tasks are like 'herding cats.'" I told my crew.

"Now do you believe what I told you about that night?"

Snow circled around me with his tail lightly flicking against me as it waved.

"Still wish you could have given us more details. Might have prevented me from almost drowning," I said. "But, yes, you got tossed overboard and were lucky enough to find some scrap plywood nearby. You said the boat capsized though."

"That's not what it's called when someone gets thrown overboard?" His whiskers twitched.

"No! It's called getting thrown overboard!" I laughed.

"Or, if you're a pirate, you might make someone walk the plank instead," Moony said.

I whipped around to face my brother. "How do you know so much about pirates?"

"I told you—the internet! You can find out anything there. And it's always right!" He licked his lips and puffed out his chest. "It also said I'm the greatest cat of all time."

"As if!" Ziti prowled toward him, then she gave him an affectionate lick on the cheek.

Priss was off in the distance, flirting with Ice. Looked like Moony had made his choice, and Priss had moved on to fairer seas. Hank was still Hank. Daisy was trying to capture a cricket. Amber and Sass were helping Cool make his way over to me.

"Hey, Mr. Cool Cat," I greeted my old friend. "How've you been feeling?"

"Oh, I'm perfectly fine," he said, stretching his paws out. "Perfectly fine. These two pretty ladies have been flirting with me all night, so I think I may even get lucky!"

We all laughed.

"I'm the lucky one." I glanced around at all my friends and family. It was fun to go on an adventure with Cat and the other bipeds. It was *really* fun to solve another mystery. But in the end, I liked being right here at home in the courtyard with my clowder. And I didn't foresee anything ever changing that.

"Who's ready for a hunt?" I asked, and all ears perked up. Paws rose into the air.

We would feast tonight. Beware, rodentia of Fairytale Forest!

CATHERINE

Gloria and I arrived in the conference room on the top floor of Guest Services to a warm greeting from Mr. and Mrs. Forest, Sheri, Karen, Derek from Security, and Jayden and Nora. "Hey, everyone!"

"You did it again, Catherine!" Mr. Forest cheered, and everyone broke out into applause.

"Well, I couldn't have done it without Gloria, Jayden and Nora. We make a great team, guys!" They all gathered around me for a group hug. I wasn't a touchy-feely kind of person, but I was here for this.

"We do make a great team," Jayden agreed, "but, unfortunately, it's my last day of work for the summer. I have to pack up and move into my dorm this weekend. School starts next week—can you believe it?"

"It's been one heck of a summer." Mr. Forest sighed as he wrapped his arm around his wife. "I really hope this is the end of *this* kind of excitement here in the park."

"Me too," Mrs. Forest agreed. "I'm so glad we were able to keep it out of the press this time. I think it helped that the murder didn't actually take place in the park, but I still can't believe the body was found here in broad daylight, and we managed to keep it hidden from guests. It's a miracle!"

"Well, that is one magical thing about Fairytale Forest," Mr. Forest said. "Guests come here expecting the unexpected—but there are some things that are so far off their radar, it doesn't even register when they do show up."

We all laughed, and then our laughter was interrupted by a knock on the conference room door. Mr. Forest's administrative assistant walked in with Detective Towers.

She came right over to me and shook my hand. "Thank you so much for helping us with the case, Ms. Lyon."

I totally solved the case—it wasn't just help—but I wasn't about to say a word. When I looked over at Gloria, she made a buttoning her lip gesture, and I grinned.

"We were able to get a confession from Mr. Morris, and he pled guilty to reckless homicide. He really thought his nephew had started a cult." She shook her head. "He and his wife were convinced Kevin had indoctrinated their son, and that's why Stevie stole the boat. They were afraid he was going to keep leveling up to bigger and more serious crimes after that."

"Kevin's own parents didn't seem to know about it. If Cassidy hadn't told her mom...who knows if any of this would have happened," I theorized.

Detective Towers nodded. "He did manage to hide it very well from his parents. After Cassidy spilled the beans, they started talking to some of the kids who played Kevin's game at the store and found out some disturbing stuff. When Stevie took the boat without permission, that was the final straw. I guess he lost his shoe trying to get the boat out of the shallows. That broke the case wide open—him and his fancy shoes."

"Yeah, and keeping Kevin's dagger didn't exactly help his case!" Gloria pointed out.

"We matched the blood on the dagger to Kevin," the detective shared. "So it was pretty cut and dried after that. He ended up telling us the whole story, most of which matched what Jayden recorded on his phone. Except the part about Kevin wrestling the dagger away and falling overboard. Apparently, Kevin's cat is still missing. I'm guessing it didn't survive."

Well, we knew better. Snow may have used one of his nine lives, but he could happily live out the other eight as part of the park's cat colony. "Did you speak with Kevin's parents after Steve was arrested?" I asked the detective. "I'm thinking the situation has caused a huge rift in their family, right?"

She nodded. "They were absolutely devastated all over again. I felt really bad for them—they seemed like nice people. Well, his stepmom is a bit eccentric, but... Oh, she was really worried about Kevin's cat. She described him as pure white with a ringed tail and blue eyes—you know, in case he did manage to survive. But he probably didn't."

Gloria and I looked at each other knowingly, then both gave a shrug. "Huh, hope he turns up," Gloria said.

Mrs. Forest clapped her hands together to get everyone's attention. "I'm glad you're all here because I have a surprise for you!" She walked over to a table in the back of the room and whipped a plastic tablecloth off to reveal a huge sheet cake. It was vanilla with sprinkles and purple writing that said,

"Good luck at C of C, Jayden! And congrats to our Fairy-tale Forest Sleuths, Cat and Gloria!"

There was a tiny purple cat next to my name.

I'd like to think it was meant to be Zoe…my feline partner in solving crime.

Epilogue

"Drat! Foiled again!" I put down the remote to my drone and kicked the door to my office shut. I looked out over the Ashley River in the direction of the wretched theme park.

My drone had just confirmed the park was operating smoothly. There had been no closures and absolutely zero press about Kevin Morris's murder.

When I planted the idea in his uncle's head that his nephew had recruited his son into a dangerous cult, he really took the bait.

I expected big things from you, Steve.

Now you've let me down.

But not to worry. I had connections to employees all over that park, and I knew I could convince someone else to go postal.

Or would it be "parkal"?

My evil laugh echoed down the hallway as I went outside to collect my drone. The thick late-summer humidity sucked the air out of my lungs, but I knew everything was about to change. Soon there would be a bit of crispness in the air. Fall was coming.

And with it would come my next target.

THE END

Follow all of Cat and Zoe's adventures:
Felines of Fairytale Forest

Join my newsletter for updates, giveaways and more!
Bit.ly/KLMontgomerynews

About the Author

K.L. Montgomery writes bodypositive sweet romance, romcom, and cozy mystery. A librarian in a former life, she now also works as an editor and runs the 6000-member Indie Author Support group on Facebook in addition to publishing under two names.

Though she remains a Hoosier at heart, K.L. shares her coastal Delaware home with some furry creatures and her husband, who is on the furry side as well. She has an undying love for her three sons, Broadway musicals, the beach, Seinfeld, the color teal, IU basketball, paisleys, and dark chocolate.

Plot Twist

Badge Bunny

Wedding War

Stage Mom

Shark Bite

Contemporary Romance Standalones

Given to Fly

The Light at Dawn

Reconstructed Heart

Women's Fiction

Fat Girl

Green Castles

Nonfiction

The Fat Girl's Guide to Loving Your Body